# RIVERENZA

# A Story of Love and Life

## M. Carolina Bento

*For my family:*
*A lineage of brave women before us,*
*our great-grandmothers, grandmothers,*
*mothers and daughters!*

## CHAPTER ONE

# IN THE PRESENT

Blythe Lisvane dedicated her professional life to the study of humans and the behaviors of ancient societies and present cultures.

Originally a Welsh-U.K. citizen, she immigrated to the United States twenty-eight years ago upon being invited by one of the most renowned universities in Boston, Massachusetts, to join its Anthropology Department as a professor and researcher.

That opportunity came at the most important time of her life, when she was ready to start a journey of her own, on her own.

After her arrival in Boston, she told Robyn, her best friend and fellow professor, she didn't come only for her professional advancement, she was pregnant and wanted to provide a life for her child away from Wales and everyone to whom she had been connected there.

She stated that in starting a new life she was erasing her past history, completely.

To Robyn, that sounded startling, but she didn't question Blythe's explanation, instead she supported her in adapting to the new city and the new job.

She also helped her find a place to live not far from the University and remained a very close friend throughout her pregnancy.

Blythe's baby girl Sabrina was born perfect and beautiful. But she would not grow up like most children, she would never experience the closeness or love of a father.

As Sabrina grew up, her mother would often say that life had begun the day her daughter was born.

Blythe bestowed on her little girl all of her love and attention, splitting her time wisely between her career and being the most involved and caring mother she could be.

During Sabrina's childhood years Blythe would tell her daughter many fascinating stories, but none of them were about her personal history, they were mostly mythological tales of ancient civilizations.

She would also describe the country from where she came, Wales, and she would speak of the natural beauty of the land and its history. Her narrative lacked any personal recounting of people or any family she had left behind. But she had mentioned that she immigrated to the U.S. because she didn't belong there...

From time to time Sabrina, a naturally curious child, would ask her mother questions about her original family and about her father. She would receive the same answer, *'It is just the two of us, darling, we have no one else! You are my only family.'* She could clearly see a veil of sadness in her mother's eyes.

As Blythe continued evading responses, over time Sabrina perceived that her mother's past was a sensitive matter that she obviously didn't want to discuss or chose to forget. In respect of her mother's feelings she gave up asking her, and eventually she let it go, hoping that someday her mother would tell her about her previous life in Wales.

The fact that Sabrina was an only child didn't seem to affect her, apparently she didn't miss out on having an extended family. Blythe had friends that became part of her daughter's life: her best friend and Sabrina's godmother Robyn, other colleagues, and the people at the daycare center in the University that cared for her as a baby.

Ma Robyn, as little Sabrina would call her godmother, loved her like her own and had a significant role in her upbringing.

For many years Blythe lived with her daughter in a small basement apartment in the city. She worked tirelessly, she had a life plan to buy a house, and she would tell her young daughter frequently:

*'Mommy is saving money to buy a beautiful house for us.'*

At age forty she was self-assured, upbeat, independent, and that was the example she wanted to give to her daughter.

*'To stand on your own, not depending emotionally or financially on anyone.'*

The time came when Blythe was able to make her dream come true. In addition to the savings from the royalties from her didactic books, she used her spare time to generate extra income as a corporate anthropologist, executing reports in market research and analysis for businesses or companies.

She brought her daughter to the historic Beacon Hill neighborhood. It was a memorable day by the end of summer when autumn was just beginning and there was an abundant mix of summer greens and fall foliage all around.

As they walked hand in hand through the aged cobblestone streets, Blythe emphatically remarked on the beauty of the attached, old brick houses with colorful doorways and window boxes filled with plants and flowers. Her enthusiasm for that neighborhood was contagious.

*'This is the city's beauty at its finest!'*

They arrived at a very narrow one way street, Wetherill Place, with attached brick homes on both sides, and joyfully she announced:

*'This is it, Bri! Our house is that one with the red door.'*

Sabrina ran to the front door.

Their dream life started on that unforgettable day…

Sabrina was nine years old when they moved in. That was the day when she met Luciana, a girl her own age, living right across the street.

The two girls connected immediately and became best friends.

They shared many commonalities, they were both born and raised in Boston, the only children of immigrants and first generation Americans.

The only difference was that Luciana had both her parents, and Sabrina only her mother.

The Monsaraz family, Manuela and Pedro, Luciana's parents, came from Portugal.

Blythe started improving their home, she taught Sabrina to help remove old wallpaper and paint walls. They had fun and a big mess for months…

The following summer Blythe brought a new friend home, Shelton, a University researcher. He also helped with the renovations and sometimes would stay overnight.

Dr. Shelton Romes, a neuropsychologist, had collaborated on some of Blythe's projects. They had long conversations, some aspects of their professional interests intertwined. They started out as colleagues but eventually they became close friends. Shelton was a clever man with great insights into human nature.

Soon Sabrina realized that he was her mother's boyfriend, and that brought her hope that her mother would marry Shelton and he would become her father. But getting married was not in Blythe's plans, she wanted to maintain her independence.

Nevertheless they truly loved each other and had a close relationship lasting for the past seventeen years. They did not even move in together as Shelton had many times proposed, but he never gave up on his commitment.

He was kind and attentive to Sabrina, always present and engaged in her life, and she learned to love him too.

Over the years, the three of them shared many good experiences together, such as holiday celebrations, graduations, or walking by the bank of the Charles River close to home, visiting sites right there in Boston, or going to the beach on summer weekends, enjoying long walks on the sand, and mostly the beautiful sunsets...

Shelton was the one who taught Sabrina how to swim and to be mindful of the ocean's strength.

There were many occasions when they would go up New England's coast, where the ocean would crash on the rocks, when Sabrina would observe her mother's melancholic look gazing at the water, sitting there for hours with her eyes lost in the distance, and she would ask her mother if she was sad.

*'No, darling! I just love to look at the ocean, it does not end there on the horizon... There is so much more after that line, other lands, other people...'*

Blythe could not have been more loving or caring to her daughter. On several occasions she brought her daughter along to conferences all over the country. Sabrina never missed out on anything, she grew up confident, adoring her mother and proud of her professional successes, prestige and recognition among her peers, and also of her beauty, her perfect facial features, beautiful brown eyes sparkled with honey, full lush brown chestnut hair, the softest olive toned skin. In all aspects, her mother was her role model.

*'We are the Bly-Bri team, an invincible duo, nothing can defeat us. Together we can do anything!'*

Sabrina and Luciana became inseparable, in perfect camaraderie they bonded like sisters. They went to the same high school and college together while they both continued living at home.

After graduating from college Luciana chose to get a job at an insurance company, following her father's footsteps, and Sabrina went straight to law school to pursue a career in international business, with her mother's full support.

Currently, at twenty-seven years old, Sabrina has a demanding job as a corporate lawyer at a renowned firm in downtown Boston.
She was promoted three years ago upon graduating, after interning for that same firm during the duration of her years in law school.

Sabrina has been dating Tom, also a lawyer, for almost two years. They have common professional goals and she enjoys his company. She believes that their easy and fun relationship is going in a serious direction.
Through it all she continued living at home with her mother, who provided her with an exceptionally good life, lovingly giving her examples of strength and resilience, until now when something changed... These past months her mother's health has deteriorated.

Concerned about Blythe's frequent and debilitating headaches and other symptoms to the point that occasionally she had blurred vision and sometimes slurred speech, which impaired her ability of enjoying the end of the year celebrations like they used to, Sabrina insisted on helping her mother find another doctor, a specialist.
Blythe minimized her symptoms, saying that her old migraines had become a little more severe lately, but she was taking care of it.

One evening in the coldest month of January, when Blythe was hurriedly typing on her computer, which was not unusual since she was always involved in research or a new study, her daughter noticed a bottle of pills on her desk and showed her concern.
"Mom, these are controlled drugs! That's what they prescribed for your migraines?"
"Yes, darling, my doctor assured me that I will need it only for a while... It is helping me now."
"Mom, I have insisted, now I am getting really concerned, I would like to come with you to see a doctor, we need a second opinion on these pills."

"Don't worry, Bri, I'll be alright, it is of great importance to me to finish writing this, I still have a long way to go."

"What is it, Mom, another publication? It can wait, you need to take care of yourself first, you look so tired, please go rest."

"Darling, you are worrying too much, I have an urgency to write this one now! It is not work, it is about my life, our lives, about things that I haven't told you and answers to questions that you asked me and I evaded responding…"

"Mom, you are scaring me! What could be so urgent? Why are you writing it? Talk to me! Maybe you'll feel better if you tell me what's on your mind. And if you don't feel like it now, we will talk tomorrow."

"Tonight I want to tell you just this, Sabrina. I can't hold back any longer… Actually I was not originally from Wales as I told everyone, I am from Greece."

"That's it, Mom? You were born in Greece and moved to Wales! That's not unusual, people move around all the time, it is not that important. I don't understand why you would keep it a secret."

"Because the reasons that made me move were very disturbing, and I did not want you to be overwhelmed by my wretched stories. I wanted you to grow up carefree and happy. I know from my own experience that memories of childhood, good or bad, will last a lifetime!"

"Mom, you gave me the best and happiest childhood, I only have good memories, but you don't have to protect me anymore, I am an adult, and above all I am your friend, there is nothing you would tell me that I would hold against you."

"I know, Bri, you are the sweetest daughter. Honestly, until now I made an effort in silencing recollections of what happened to me before I came to America, in an attempt to protect myself, but most of all I did not want to bring any burden upon you or create doubts in your mind. I was afraid that I would shock you… It was always my deepest desire that you would grow up happy, without worries, and most of all emotionally independent and free.

Forgive me, darling, but I need to stop now, I am feeling very tired."

"It's alright, Mommy, we will talk more tomorrow, and don't forget, I want to accompany you to your doctor to discuss this medication, maybe it is doing you more harm than good."

Blythe held on to her daughter's arm and walked to her room.

That night Sabrina was extremely worried about her mother's obvious health issue and puzzled about what she had told her, and she was curious to know more. She was prepared to listen to her mother without preconceived judgment, she truly believed that her mother had justifiable reasons for not telling her earlier.
She had a restless night.

The next morning surprisingly Blythe looked fine and assured her daughter that she felt much better, the headache was gone and she was going to her office at the University and would call her doctor for an appointment.

Sabrina left for work.

In the evening when she arrived at home, her mother had come earlier and was already writing.
"I had a much better day, Bri, no headache at all!"
"That's great, Mom! Did you make a doctor's appointment anyway?"
"Yes, for Thursday. But you don't have to come with me, I'm perfectly capable of doing this alone, and I know how busy you are, darling."

After dinner Blythe continued writing.
Sabrina asked her, "Do you feel like telling me about Greece tonight, Mom? I am anxious to know more!"
"Yes, let me finish this page, darling."

A little later…
"Let's have some tea and talk, Bri."

Sabrina brought tea upstairs to her Mom's room and sat on her bed.
"I must tell you once more, darling, that my life, as you know, started when you were born. In many ways we grew up together.

When you arrived I left my past behind, I did not dwell on it any longer, but through it all there was a place in my heart where I kept many memories and the love for my homeland, for my mother and my brother."

"Did you have a brother, Mom?"

"Yes, Demetrius, we used to call him Dimitri. I lost him, it was cruel… That's why I ended up in Wales, alone."

Blythe paused, sipped some tea, then continued.

"I was born in a remote village that doesn't show up on any map. My home was a rudimentary but magical place where I had a beautiful and innocent childhood until I was seventeen years old, when my brother and I were sent to school in England!

I was very attached to my family, and to this day I carry one regret… That I never went back to be reunited with my loved ones, in spirit."

"You were in England, before going to Wales, Mom?"

"Yes, darling, I spent almost two years in London, then I lived in Wales for twelve years until I was thirty-two years old, when I finally learned the lessons that life had given me and became self-reliant. But to accomplish it I deliberately obliterated my earlier weaknesses, dependency and the events that changed the course of my life."

"Mom, this is not clear to me, it is confusing… For what I know you were never weak or dependent."

"I was not always, darling, but it is your birthright to know your heritage, who I was, where I came from, where you came from…

I came to realize that all had a purpose and I am revealing to you the truth with unflinching certainty that this is the right time, the only time!"

Sabrina's heart sank.

"Mom, why are you making a point that this is the only time? What do you mean?"

"I have been agonizing about it, Bri, honestly I should have told you sooner. I am so sorry I didn't, I was afraid you would be troubled by the events and the choices I made, and I would lose your respect, and also that in recounting past facts my heart would break and I would become weak again…"

"Mom, you have nothing to apologize for, I will never judge or criticize your decisions. For me you have always been the strongest and fairest person I know."

"You are a remarkable young woman that I had the privilege to love and raise with much pride. My daughter, you brought abundant miracles and gifts into my life. I am a professor but you have been my teacher, showing me the wonder of being a child, the hope, the trust that life ahead has a myriad of possibilities.

I believe now that everything in life had and has a reason... I am free of my past angst and it is my purpose to give you true answers. I feel indebted to you, Bri, that's why I am revealing the story of my life in Greece and Wales.

I only ask you to understand why I chose to do what I did. Sometimes under daring circumstances we don't feel we have any other option but to rewrite a whole new script for our lives to be able to continue living."

Blythe became emotional. Sabrina hugged her.

"Mom, Mommy, you look so sad, you don't have to continue talking now."

"That's why I decided to write everything, Bri, the emotions take over me, and I need to remain objective."

"We can continue tomorrow, Mom. I am looking forward to hear your story, and I hope that you are going to tell me also about my father."

"Yes, darling, I am going to give you the truth, the entire truth, but for now you should know that he was a good man, he loved me and I loved him! If circumstances were different you would have had the best father... I am sorry, Bri."

Her voice was breaking.

"I'm alright, Mom, I have the best mother!"

Blythe reached for a pill.

"Remember, Bri, love crosses all boundaries, our souls are connected for eternity. I love you forever, my sweet daughter."

"I love you forever, Mommy. Sleep well."

Sabrina went to her room overwhelmed with emotions and concerns, she never saw her mother in such a fragile emotional state, expressing her feelings that way. She was intrigued by her words and anxious to continue their conversation the next day.

In the morning Blythe looked well, ready to start a new day.

Sabrina was surprised to see her mother apparently in good disposition.

"I am glad you are feeling better this morning, Mom, but I was thinking maybe all you need is a break, a medical leave to de-stress and get rid of the migraines. What do you think, Mom?"

"I have thought of that, I'll discuss it with Dr. Newman."

They both left for their jobs, like on any other ordinary day...

Later that afternoon, unexpectedly, Sabrina got a call from the Anthropology Department informing her that her mother had been taken to the hospital. She had a seizure and collapsed in her office, and her assistant called the paramedics.

Sabrina rushed to the hospital, just a few blocks away from her law firm, where her mother was being evaluated and undergoing tests.

The attendants at the Emergency Department told her that her mother's doctor was discussing the patient's status with the medical staff, and he would come out to talk to her, momentarily.

She waited for an agonizing hour until he came and took her to a private office.

"I am Dr. Newman, and I am sorry we are meeting under these circumstances."

"What's happening to my Mom, Dr. Newman?"

"This is very serious, Sabrina. Three months ago your mother was diagnosed with an intracranial tumor. She knew of her condition."

Sabrina felt dizzy, like she couldn't feel the floor under her feet.

"A brain tumor? Did she know all along?"

"It is fast growing and inoperable, in other words life threatening. She has been evaluated by the best oncologist and neurosurgeon, unfortunately there was nothing to be done...

Sabrina, this outcome was predictable but it came sooner than we expected. I am sorry to tell you, you need to prepare yourself, your mother is in a coma, on life support..."

She felt like she was punched in the gut, she couldn't assimilate what she was hearing.

"Life support? Can I see my Mom? Is she in pain?"

"You can see her, briefly. She is sedated, she won't feel pain again. Do you have anyone that could take you home? You need to rest to face what is to come…"

"What's to come?"

"We will talk tomorrow. Last time I saw Blythe she told me she was planning to take a medical leave to spend more time with you and tell you everything. She has made arrangements… I have a copy of her living will in my office, you might find the original at home."

Dr. Newman guided her to the ICU.

Sabrina's heart shattered when she saw her mother hooked up to monitors, pale and lifeless, she didn't look like the lively woman that left the house just that morning.

After a while a nurse came in and gently asked her to leave and return in the morning. There was nothing she could do for her mother.

She went home alone, her thoughts were scattered, she was devastated, trying to make sense of everything that was happening.

She did not call anyone, not even Luciana or her godmother Robyn, now retired and living in Cape Cod.

A little later Shelton called her. He heard that Blythe was in the hospital.

"I'm upset, I called the hospital, they didn't give me any information about Blythe's condition. Please tell me, Sabrina, how is she?"

Sabrina told him of the situation and spoke of her disbelief of her mother's condition.

Shelton, also staggered, said he had sensed something was very wrong, he had witnessed Blythe's sharp decline for the past couple of months, along with her intense and severe headaches, dizziness and loss of balance.

"We all noticed, I insisted to go to the doctor with her, but she already knew, she didn't want to worry us. Dr. Newman told me they believed she had more time… "

"I am here for you and your Mom, count on me, Sabrina. I am devastated, you know how much I love her.
I'll come to the hospital to see you and her, tomorrow."

Sabrina couldn't sleep that night. She went to her mother's room, lay on her bed, feeling the deepest stabbing pain in her chest. She sobbed.

Early in the morning she called her godmother and told her what was happening. Robyn was also shocked with the grim news and told her she was coming to Boston immediately to be with them.
"I'll stay with Blythe at the hospital, and with you, my darling, for as long as it takes!"

Sabrina also called Luciana.
"Luci, my Mom is in the hospital, it is serious, very serious, she has a brain tumor…"
"I'll be right over, Bri!"

In a few minutes Luciana was there.
"I am not going to work today, I'll go to the hospital with you."
The two childhood friends embraced, and Sabrina broke into tears.
"Oh, Luci, the doctor said Mom is not coming back… I can't live without her, she is all the family I have. Oh, not my Mom! She doesn't deserve this!"
"She doesn't, no one does. Maybe there is hope! I'm here with you, we are sisters forever. You are not alone."

Sabrina took a deep breath and looked in her mother's desk, and in a folder she found the original will, completed and signed only eight weeks before.
Luciana was sitting at her side, and in between tears, together they read the will.
"I can't do this, Luci. She doesn't want to be kept on life support. And what about being cremated? She never discussed that issue with me. Oh, God, I can't, I can't do this!
Let's go to the hospital, I want to be with my Mom every

moment…"

As they were leaving she got a call from Robyn, "I am on the road, driving slowly, there is snow…"
"Drive safe, Ma Robyn, I'll leave the keys across the street with Manuela, Luci's Mom. I am on my way to the hospital now."

At the hospital Sabrina was allowed to sit by her mother's bedside. She controlled her emotions as much as she could, held her hand.
"Mommy, I am here, I'll do everything to make you better. Together we can do anything! You are not alone, Mommy, I love you!"

Dr. Newman came in and patiently showed her the results of the last MRI of her mother's brain and other tests disclosing the mass deeply knotted in the central neuro system.
"It is constricting the brain with a rapid increase in intracranial pressure. Your mother felt the symptoms for a long time, she didn't neglect it, initially she thought her old migraines were getting worse… After the diagnosis she went through all the steps and consulted with the oncologist and neurosurgeon, but unfortunately nothing could be done. I need to tell you that she was extremely brave, she was resigned to her fate.
Her vital functions will deteriorate fast, you need to prepare yourself, Sabrina, she didn't want to be kept on life support."
"I can't do it, Dr. Newman! I won't let my Mom go."
"Let's wait a couple of days, Sabrina. I'll be around, the other doctors will keep you informed. We are all here to keep Blythe comfortable and to support you."

Sabrina felt like she was living in a nightmare. All of a sudden her world was turned upside down, from having a loving mother one day to seeing her dying the next, without being able to do anything to help her. It was unbearable!

Shelton came in later, sat with Sabrina and cried.
"You know I love your Mom, she is my soulmate. She has been a major part of my life, and I want to share what is to come with

14

you, I am here for both of you."
Sabrina leaned her head on his shoulder and cried with him.
"Mom has loved you since I was ten years old and I love you too. I need you, Shelton, we can do this together for her, until the end…"

Robyn arrived, while Shelton went to get her at Blythe's house, Luciana stayed with Sabrina in the hospital.

Sabrina called her boyfriend to inform him of what was happening. He didn't show any empathy, only said that hospitals were not the environment he liked to be in and there was nothing he could do to help, anyway…
She was stunned that in that crucial moment Tom was not emotionally available to her, but she didn't waste any thoughts on him, all of her attention was placed on her mother.
He did not come to the hospital, not even once, to see her.

Minutes, hours, days seemed to drag, Sabrina felt she was running against time, she didn't leave her Mom's bedside and she spoke to the other doctors. Patiently they described in detail her mother's hopeless condition.
Her friends Luciana, Robyn and Shelton took turns keeping her company on her vigil.

A week later the doctors informed her the end was near… Her mother's vital signs were fading away, and on that cold and dreary afternoon, Blythe expired, naturally, quietly, while Sabrina was whispering words of love, "Mommy, I won't leave you, I love you forever."
Sabrina was paralyzed by the devastation.
Robyn held her.
"Your Mom is free from suffering, she is in peace."
She did not find any comfort in those words, her heart was shattered, she felt her mother's passing very deeply, she thought she would never recover from losing the only family she ever had, and the one that she most loved and admired.
She told herself that nothing, not even death, would ever rip her Mom out of her heart. Never!

After the funeral service at the University Auditorium where hundreds of people celebrated Blythe's life, Sabrina tried to comfort Shelton, he looked defeated, the light of that vivacious man had gone out. He was the one who had stood by them over the years, giving her and her mother countless demonstrations of love. She felt sorry for him, and for a moment she forgot her own pain.

Robyn decided to stay a few more days with her. Sabrina didn't talk much during the first days, she just wanted to sleep and forget that her mother was not there anymore... Not even the sweetest words or the loving hugs of her friend took her pain away, she thought she would never overcome the sorrow of that immensurable loss. It all seemed surreal.

Tom, her boyfriend, finally showed up at home.
"Are you feeling better, Sabrina? Sorry, there was nothing I could do."
"You could have supported me, Tom, in what I am going through, this is immensely painful. Feeling better? That's all you can say? I don't even have the energy to talk about it."
"I don't know what to say, Sabrina, I love you and I just want to cheer you up, I think it is best if we don't talk about worries or sadness."
She felt hurt and told him at that point her main priority was taking care of her mother's affairs and that she had no expectations that he could understand her devastation, nor support her in overcoming her grief. She had no disposition to continue talking and asked him to leave.

But she was not alone, she was thankful to have Robyn and Shelton present, comforting her and one another through that difficult time.

In the Sunday newspaper, Robyn pointed out an obituary.
"Look, Sabrina, it is about your Mom:
'Blythe Lisvane, a highly accomplished and admired professor of our academic community, a true friend to so many, and a loving and devoted mother, has passed away at age sixty. She is survived by her only daughter Sabrina. She will be profoundly missed.'"

"Ma Robyn, I don't know how I am going to survive without her... My Mom was my world, a part of me, I feel like my heart has been ripped out, I can't live without her."

"You can and you will, darling, you are like her, you can do anything! I remember clearly when she accepted the invitation to come to our University, as she arrived she gave me the news that she was pregnant with you!

Can you imagine a thirty-two year old woman starting a new life alone, in a new country, with a baby? She was so brave!"

"She was, until the end... Ma Robyn, in her last days she said some things, she told me she was not Welsh, she was Greek! Did she ever tell you anything like this?"

"To tell you the truth, once Blythe told me that she was born in Greece, I didn't think much of it, maybe her family had immigrated to the U.K. You know how reserved she was, she didn't say anything else."

"Mom was writing about her life history, she was in a rush to tell me, she felt compelled to answer my childhood questions about her, her family, my father... I have wondered, of course, but I didn't press the issue in respect of her privacy. One of these days I'll gather the courage to start looking into it, right now I feel broken."

"I understand, darling. While we were at the hospital, Shelton commented that Blythe had suffered great trauma when she was young, he believed that as a consequence of not dealing with it her body reacted with chronic headaches..."

"Trauma? I know nothing about it. I feel so sorry for Shelton, he loved my Mom, and I am sure he tried to help her. I will talk to him opportunely, maybe he knows more."

Before Robyn went back to Cape Cod, Sabrina asked her to take Scotty, her mother's dog, along.

"I don't think I can take care of him, he misses Mom too. He is going to be lonely here while I am at work."

"I love Scotty, I'll be glad to have him, and you can come to see us often, Bri, you'll always have a place in my home and my heart."

"And you in mine. I also will be researching when and where to bring my Mom's ashes, as she asked me in her will.

*'Please, on your time, bring me home to Greece. I want to be reunited with my family, in Mother Earth's womb...'"*

"Count on me if you don't want to do it alone, I would take a trip to Greece for Blythe, with you."

Sabrina spoke to Shelton and invited him to come for coffee.
"If you feel comfortable coming back to our house."
"Of course, I have many happy memories of Blythe's home."

He came.
"I'm missing her so very much, it hurts. And it gives me comfort to look at you and see her, young and vibrant! Blythe will live in you, her daughter, you were the best part of her, the light of her life. She was very proud of you, Sabrina."

"And I was proud of my Mom, so proud. She was accomplished, prolific, caring, generous, but also secretive... She mentioned things about her past in her final days and she left me something in writing.

Did Mom confide in you, Shelton? Please tell me what you know."

"I agree, Sabrina, she was secretive, I just accepted the little information she offered me. Many times during our ample discussions about human behaviors I expected her to open up and reveal some of her own life experiences, but she always restricted any personal history.

It was obvious to me that she had been traumatized earlier. I must say that no one would erase the past so dramatically as she did for no reason other than having suffered from a deeply disturbing event.

Over a month ago Blythe was having one of those bad days with a debilitating headache when, unexpectedly, she told me she was getting ready to tell you her whole life story. She didn't do it before because she wanted you to grow up free of worries and never suffer any trauma like she did, when at a young age she lost her entire family in a very brutal manner.

She was alone in the world and found a home in Wales with her first love, your father. Eventually, she decided to leave to start a new life. I assumed he had died...

She ingrained herself in the American way of life, expecting that the memories of her troubled past would be forgotten. They weren't, and many times she felt tormented.

That's all I know. Blythe became obviously distressed talking about it, there was great sadness in her eyes. She was quite vulnerable, and I didn't question her any further.

I know quite well that the shock of a life altering event might lead survivors of trauma to denial, and they may become disconnected, but living with emotional issues such as sadness, anxiety and guilt, for a lifetime."

"Shelton, that's why she didn't want to share her history with me! She would open old wounds recounting it. Now that she is not here she left me the answers.

I feel so deeply sorry for my Mom, for her losses. Strangely I feel like in disclosing those events I would be intruding into a past that she guarded so carefully."

"Take your time, Sabrina, first you need to heal.

Remember, she was completely happy with you, she used to say you were a gift from Heaven and a blessing."

"Shelton, thank you for understanding how I feel, it helps me a great deal talking to you. Please count on me too, we both need to heal..."

"Blythe was and still is the best part of my life, and I am glad we are on this path together!"

"For always, Shelton, for always!"


Luciana came over.

"My Mom and I were talking and we don't think you should be here alone, come live with us, Bri, at least for now."

"I appreciate it, Luci, but I need to face and adjust to my new life, and I also have a lot to do here, organizing Mom's things, hundreds of books, papers, documents, and read and research... I don't have the energy now to read Mom's writings, but I'll do it when I am strong enough not to fall apart."

"I understand, Bri, and I profoundly feel it, but I think you need to overcome your grief, to learn what's still to come without breaking into pieces. It is just too many emotions at the same time."

Sabrina placed the urn, a little wooden box with her Mom's

ashes, on the desk in her Mom's bedroom and locked the door.

Her head was spinning, she was overwhelmed feeling her mother's unending absence.

'I miss you, Mom, I wish I could see you, hear your voice again.'

She locked the door and went to her room.

She fell asleep between tears…

Sabrina resumed work, grateful for the tolerance and time that was given to her to attend to her mother and to grieve. But grieving was not over, it was going to be a long process.

She directed the issues of her mother's estate in the care of a lawyer and decided to throw herself at work like never before.

For the next couple of months that is what she did, but not even for a moment she forgot her Mom, her loving presence, her warmth, her wisdom. Sometimes she felt Blythe was still there, she heard her voice echoing through the house, calling her name. For seconds she thought she heard her Mom's footsteps coming down the stairs, she was delighted thinking she would see her again, would hear her melodic voice adding unusual words to the conversation… Sabrina smiled remembering her Mom's particularly unique style of expressing herself.

One of the things that her mother always did with great enthusiasm was to celebrate spring's arrival, planting in the flower pots by the front door and filling the house with fresh flowers.

After the most cold and devastating winter, Sabrina bought many yellow flowers, her Mom's favorite, to celebrate her most appreciated season. She went to her room to air it, opened the shades, letting the sunlight in, dusted it all up, placed the urn by a round table under the window and arranged the flowers.

"For you, Mommy, with all my love!"

She shed a tear.

"I am trying to replace tears with smiles when I think of you, Mom. You left me a lifetime of beautiful, loving memories, so many… You taught me so much, I feel gratitude for our lives together, and honoring you I choose to be resilient. Oh, but how I miss you, Mommy!"

Days later, Luciana took her out for dinner.
"It's your birthday, Bri! Let's celebrate, sister!"
"Oh my, I almost forgot! I am twenty-eight!"

She hadn't seen Tom since the winter, but he had called her a couple of times to check on her, unexpectedly he invited her out. She met him after work.

He was a little awkward, it was apparent that he did not want to talk about the events of her life, he only wanted to distract her, motivating her to go dancing or maybe spending the night with him.

"We have been apart for too long, and I miss you, Sabrina, I miss what we had before, we had so much fun together."

"I agree, Tom, but life is not only about fun, there are the happy and the sad moments, and in a true relationship we share them all."

"You know me! I prefer to share the happy times!"

She felt he was insensitive and wouldn't acknowledge her feelings.

She told him he had not an ounce of empathy in his heart, he was unable to understand what she was dealing with for the past few months, and she was not able to enjoy his company like before...

She let him go.

In late spring, on a sunny weekend, Sabrina went to visit Robyn in Cape Cod. They have spoken often, but she hadn't seen her godmother since the winter.

Talking to her was somewhat like having her mother again, sharing a loving and empathetic conversation.

She also felt for Robyn, she too hurt for the loss of her best friend. Those two women had much affinity, they shared common interests for so long.

Sabrina was glad to see Scotty, she was afraid he was feeling abandoned by her, but he was terribly excited seeing her.

"I miss him, I think he thinks I am his sister. Mom used to treat him like he was her baby."

"He is happy here, Bri, and I am happy having him. But tell me about you, darling. How are you feeling?"

"It hurts very much, I miss Mom terribly. I have thrown myself at work all day, but at home alone I can hardly function. I couldn't even start taking care of Mom's things.

But, Mom raised me to be strong, and in her honor I am trying to get through it, getting ready to start reading what she was writing in her last weeks. I hope I'll find closure knowing how Mom lived her life before me."

"You will, darling! By the way, Shelton called me, he has been very lonely too and worried about you."

"I know, we talk all the time, he is so caring! He lost his relationship with Mom but he did not let go of his 'father figure' role! He came the other day to ask me if I needed any financial help. Fortunately, I don't need anything, the house has been fully paid with the insurance, plus some other income that I'm still getting from the University.

I am fine, I have my job, all I need is the love and support that I keep getting from you and him. I also have Luciana and her mother pushing me forward, I am not alone. I will overcome! I'll do it for my Mom, for her to be in peace."


Returning home, she was feeling stronger, let the light in the house and decided not to be overwhelmed by the stressful silence. She felt ready to start her journey into her mother's past.


Later Sabrina searched her mother's computer and found a file labeled, *'Greece – My Home.'*
Her heart told her:
'This is the one! I am ready!'
She printed it and started reading.

CHAPTER TWO

# GREECE - MY HOME
### by Blythe Lisvane

*I* was born in a remote area of Evia, also known by the ancient name of Euboea, the second largest island in Greece.

There was much to be seen on the island full of interesting places displaying a rich variety of archaeological sites, quiet old villages, as well as agricultural towns, farms and orchards.

Evia's topography was as diverse as anywhere else in Greece, and it was long in extension, stretching from the Pelion Peninsula to the coast of Attica. The mountainous interior featured fertile valleys, rich forests, wooded mountainsides, an abundance of crystal clear streams and some hidden, almost inaccessible places.

The southern point was a very short distance from the Cycladic Islands.

The west coast close to the mainland was separated by a narrow strait, easily accessible by a road and bridge, and was only a short drive away from Athens. Due to its proximity by land, many perceived it as being part of the mainland, barely counting Evia as an island.

The island's capital Chalkida, also known as Chalkis, located right across the bridge, was a cosmopolitan city with many businesses and a defined charm with many attractions and places to visit.

The coast offered magnificent sandy beaches with crystal clear waters, numerous restaurants, ancient villages and seaside resorts, which made it a largely popular destination among Greeks who headed there in considerable numbers on weekends or for summer vacations.

There were well kept roadways coming out of Chalkis for access to the north, south or across the island to the east coast, offering an easy drive and outstanding views. However, going to smaller and distant villages off the main roads, much of the journey would be on narrow gravel ways, sometimes paths.

The North Road offered one of the most beautiful drives through mountains and forests. A spa town with natural hot water gushing from rocks and crevices into pools was one of the main attractions of that area.

The East Road went across the island all the way to the east coast, reaching the beautiful Aegean beaches with an abundance of natural coves, resorts and hidden villages with small sheltered harbors for fishing boats. Thirty-one kilometers away from Chalkis it passed through the village of Steni, located at the slopes of Mount Dirfis.

Steni was a popular location attracting many Athenians on day trips, not only for its famous meat restaurants but also to enjoy its cooler climate in the summer.

The village stood out for its rare beauty, natural crystal clear spring waters and streams running through it, and parks scattered throughout for recreation.

From the village outskirts, steep and well-maintained trails branched into the mountain, where hikers had the opportunity to explore the great forest of Dirfis and enjoy its rich nature and amazing views.

Another popular attraction in town was an outdoor market to buy and sell products from the region.

The village was not too attractive in the dreary winter months, but still it was nice enough for people to come for the clear and crisp mountain air and to enjoy a special meal.

In the far east side of the village, a well traveled road led to the central mountains. By midway on that road there was a rugged, narrow winding way to the northeast of about twelve kilometers long across the forest and mountainous slopes that ended in a valley, where the largest natural olive grove encroached in the mountainside grew wildly for centuries.

A natural waterfall and stream enriched the soil on and around the grove.

Under the olive trees and up the mountainside a profusion of *lupinus genus* and giant fennel bushes, *ferula communis*, blossomed in yellow flowers, permeating the grounds from the grove to the plateau and the cliff, bursting out of the soil in between rocks in a colorful display of natural beauty.

The *lupinus* bushes, when in bloom, before maturing in bean pods, added a beautiful purple color to the scenery.

That was where my ancestors, a mountainous nomadic group, found shelter in the natural caves, settled and populated the area centuries ago.

They took ownership of the olive grove, expanding it and making it their main source of livelihood. Over time, many others joined them.

Straight east from the grove, following a narrow walking path of more than two kilometers, on the right hillside there were caves, some natural, others carved out, and on the left, rustic houses of stone were built in a row, not visible from the sea, until reaching a plateau.

The plateau, a large flat portion of the terrain, marked a stretch of rocky cliff, in some parts not higher than fifty meters, where the most magnificent views of the tranquil and blue waters of the Aegean Sea were unobstructed.

Legend has it that on the plateau there were remnants of what appeared to be a ruin, perhaps an ancient lighthouse represented by a mount of boulders and rocks. Some of the elders doubted that anyone had been in that place before them, they believed they were the first ones in the region, and they decided to use those rocks and boulders to construct, stone by stone, what became their family home perched high above the sea.

They called it the *frurio*, the Greek word for fortress.

The *frurio* was not a fortress by any means, it was merely one large room, with only an adjacent small room for the head of the family, where the Pheris family gathered together, day and night, and enjoyed the magnificent, undisturbed views of the Aegean Sea.

Kostas, my father, was of the first Pheris generation born and raised in the *frurio*. His grandfather had finished the construction years prior to his birth.

Continuing down to the cliff on the rocky path, there was a crease with carved steps to access a very small manmade harbor.

There were no beaches on that portion of the coast, therefore it was not explored by tourists, and it was not officially graded as a village, but only as a settlement, the reason why it did not appear on any map of the region.

However, the family always called it their village and named it Pherula. As well as their last name, Pheris, it was inspired by the extraordinary abundance of *ferula communis* bushes all over the grounds.

Astoundingly, from spring to fall, the cliff wall facing the sea looked like an everlasting suspended garden of lush blooming bushes growing out of crevices in the rocks. A breathtaking view!

The stories about our village and our ancestors were passed from generation to generation by word, everything I learned about the Pheris family and Pherula I heard from my grandfather Pappous.

He told us that his great-grandfather, an intelligent man, was the one who took ownership of the land, and his grandfather, more than one hundred years before our time, was the one who adventured to the coast, settling on the plateau and starting to build the *frurio*.

According to Pappous, the brightest of all was his son Kostas, my father, who bought a small, old heavy-duty truck and started selling the products of the grove in Chalkis. Until then they were transported in baskets, in small amounts, on the backs of mules through the treacherous path to be traded in Steni.

Since a young age my father was a natural entrepreneur, he was the one managing tasks and delegating responsibilities to the villagers, some cultivating the olive grove and the *lupinus* bushes, others carving and enlarging the path to the sea with their own hands, then expanding into the small manmade port, to adventure into the waters, fishing.

Under Kostas' naturally skilled direction, the modest village prospered. After his first marriage he left the cultivation of the grove entirely up to Pappous and the villagers, and started adventuring on fishing expeditions, saying that he was *a man of the sea*.

When he returned from his expeditions he started making more improvements to the *frurio*, adding luxuries that he would bring from faraway places, never seen in that area before.

He had a son, Spiros, and about the time his son was an adolescent, Kostas' wife died of a fever that took the lives of a few villagers too. He then decided he was going to take on longer expeditions, expanded the small harbor and brought home a large fishing boat, he called it his *yacht*.

Kostas traveled quite often for long periods of time, and on one of those trips he returned home with a new wife from one of the Cycladic Islands.

In the village a couple's union was established by a verbal commitment between the potential groom with the family of the potential bride, most of the time involving a dowry, as small as a goat or sheep. But there were two conditions to be agreed upon: first the chosen bride would have to accept the groom's proposal, and second, the union was to last until the end of their lifetime.

Adina was still a teenager when she became Kostas' second wife. At seventeen she gave birth to Dimitri, my brother, and about two years later I was born! My mother named me Dinora, and my birth was well celebrated, I was the first girl after a few generations of boys in the Pheris family!

My mother, my sweet, young and loving mother, didn't know

much about the world, she was illiterate like everyone else in our village, but she had an instinctive knowledge and taught us much about respecting and appreciating what nature offered and about family unity. She repeated quite often: *'Families are stronger when they stay together, for better or for worse...'*

We hardly spent time with Spiros, our much older brother, our father would take him along on his trips across the Aegean Sea to Turkey, Syria and other places.

Father didn't talk much but he commented he had a business partner, a savvy Turkish man, whom we never met.

Once, when we were young, our father took us to a beach resort down south in his *yacht*, and we felt very spoiled. That's when, for the first time, we saw rooms with lights on the ceilings, faucets with running water, floors covered with wood or tiles, and the most incredible device: a telephone!

Mother, Dimitri and I were mesmerized. The world out there was nothing like our little world! It was wondrous!

Dimitri and I grew up very close together, as my beloved big brother he protected me and I looked up to him. Our lives were simple, filled with joy and laughter, honey, flowers and rocks, many rocks.

We were always with Mama, she had a childlike quality, she was more often like a big sister to us, playing with us around the rocks and bushes in our courtyard.

I still feel the wind and the light of the sunset on my skin, and the laughter still echoes in my ears.

My heart was happy, so happy for sharing that magical place with my brother and my mother. I loved our beautiful little village, our little world. Our home!

Somehow Mother knew and taught us the scientific names of the plants and flowers growing around, and at night she pointed to the stars and named them too.

Oh, the clear, starry skies of Evia, I never saw anything like it anywhere else in the world!

Only in low tides, a small portion of rocky sand near the harbor was exposed for a few hours. Mama would take us down on the carved steps to the sand where we would find the most amazing shells and wet our feet in the cold water of the sea. Those were precious experiences of our young lives.

Dimitri collected stones and pebbles. What else would interest a boy in a place covered with rocks!

Now, so many decades later, those memories of my childhood in my home of Pherula are vivid and present, and my heart beats melancholic!

Father would bring us gifts and goods from far off lands when he returned home. He would say that his business was growing and he was going to become one of the richest men in Greece, and his sons would continue with it! That's when he suddenly decided to send Dimitri to a boarding school in Chalkis.

He spoke firmly, Dimitri was going to be the first Pheris who would not grew up illiterate.

I held on to my brother, I didn't want him to leave, and I was very scared that my father would take him away.

We were amazed to see Mama standing up, begging him not to send Dimitri away from home. She suggested he find a teacher in Steni for us, she wanted me to be as educated as my brother.

To our surprise, Father agreed in bringing in a teacher to the *frurio* for both of us. He was so eager that he had a room built especially for our teacher Edessa.

She came to stay with us during the week, for our entire elementary education.

One of the first things she taught us was that Evia had an ancient history, and it had been colonized not only by the Greeks but also the Turks. And that in some villages like ours, the dialect spoken was so different that it was difficult to understand, and she was going to teach us the true Greek language.

She also brought us many books and pictures of other places, when we learned that the world was much bigger than our island. There were all sorts of peoples, living and speaking so differently than us. It was fascinating to learn!

What we appreciated the most was that Mama also learned to read and write at the same time with us. It was amazing to share that experience with her, always participating in our lives.

During those elementary years, several times Edessa took us to her house in Steni. She built a new house with the money my father was paying her, she said that was her main motivation for that job.

Mama allowed us to stay there from time to time, while we were learning new things. For us, Steni was a big town and very exciting, it had electricity, which was something we appreciated, and running water coming out of a faucet inside the house! It was fantastic!

As soon as we learned to read and write, Pappous asked us to start writing the stories he told us about our ancestors.

Dimitri delegated that to me, which I fully embraced, I enjoyed writing, and listening to Pappous' stories was a treat. He was happy about it and said that he knew the Pheris family stories would last for posterity.

I wrote many of them over the years.

Father decided that we would go further in our education. We understood that was a big step for a man who had never attended school, for Dimitri and me it was hard to comprehend his sudden interest in educating us, but we embraced it.

In time we came to realize that for him it was a validation of his new wealth, and it became a matter of status having children that were well spoken and learned other languages.

We knew of other languages, Edessa had told us, but she never taught us any other words besides Greek ones.

Father demanded that my brother learn English. He said he would apply his language skills expanding the family business in the future. He told Dimitri he was going to send him to an English boarding school in Chalkis.

At that time, my brother rejected the idea and told Father he was not going if it was not with me, because I was the one more interested in learning than he was.

I was hungry for learning and I couldn't bear the idea that Dimitri would go away and I wouldn't see or talk to him every day.

My father agreed that he would wait another year until I was at the age of attending that same school.

When I was thirteen years old, Edessa helped us out with the enrollment, and Mother came with us to Chalkis.

I was not happy about leaving home and my mother, but I would go anywhere with my brother.

Mama was sad for leaving us there, but at the same time proud that we were attending that school. She vowed to visit us often, which she did.

We were astonished, for the three of us Chalkis was the biggest city we ever had seen, but only until we saw Athens! On countless occasions, Mama would come with us to the mainland, a short drive away from Chalkis.

I still remember the first time we saw Athens. Magnificent! We thought of it as the largest and prettiest city in the world.

Just like us, Mama had the eyes of wonderment of a child discovering and seeing new things for the first time. That was an unforgettable time in our lives.

I found it fascinating! The rich architecture and ancient history, the people. My interest for learning about cultures, people and places became paramount. The reason why I became an anthropologist!

During our holidays we always went home to Pherula, when I decided to start teaching the young villagers. I had a plan, after completing school I would come back home and would set up a school for all, young and old, to learn our language and about our country and the world.

I made many friends at that time in our village, some of them would wait for me to come home on holidays and weekends just to be able to learn something new, and I was at my happiest sharing what I knew with them.

Our family had grown, Spiros had been married for a while and he and his wife had children, one a year, and I adored my little nephews and nieces and taught them also.

Dimitri used his vacation time to work with the men at the olive grove, he was more interested in the business aspect of selling and expanding the products of the land, olives and lupini beans.

Father and Spiros continued their frequent long travels and did not offer us any information about their business. Dimitri would ask about what he was invested in, but Father only responded, *'It was about transportation...'*

He was vague, we had no idea what he was transporting. People? Goods?

That was the time when Dimitri and I had discussions about it. I didn't think much of it, but my brother was suspicious of our father's business. He always brought so much money, and it was not from fishing, he had no fishing equipment in his boat at all. We couldn't understand where the money was coming from.

By the time Dimitri and I were completing our studies in Chalkis and I was planning to set up my little school in Pherula, Father went a step further and proudly told us that he was going to send us to a university, and he gave us the chance to chose either Athens or London!

We were astonished by Father's extraordinary decision, it was an affirmation of his limitless ambition. But at the same time we embraced the opportunity, we felt privileged. It never had crossed our minds that two children coming from such a simple, modest and unknown place would ever attend a university!

Dimitri and I were already fluent in English, and he thought that going to England would easily further our language skills, and he decided we should go to London!

He was excited, but I was frightened going on a big adventure that would take us away even further from our home and our mother. I did not want to go.

Mama in her selflessness supported us, telling us that four years would go by fast and we would always come back home on holidays and would make the best of our time together.

She was a bit sad, she told us she would miss us, but in the meantime, she would keep herself very involved with her grandchildren, four of them by that time, and also assisting Pappous, who in his old age became quiet, practically immobile.

Our mentor from our school prepared us for our life in London, in workshops she showed us slides and taught us how to get around the city. She also helped us with registration and even finding a place for us to live.

I was seventeen and heartbroken for leaving Mama behind and terribly scared of flying. Dimitri was nineteen and very excited for our first trip, reassuring me that everything was going to be alright! I could never have done it without my brother.

Our first weeks in England were certainly challenging, but our mutual support and bond held us through it all.

London was extremely different than Chalkis or Athens, initially I dreaded being on the streets alone. I felt lost, eventually I learned to walk from the apartment to the school. I started enjoying my new surroundings and developed a feeling of gratitude for that magnificent opportunity of being a college student, something that was almost impossible for a girl like me to even have imagined.

Dimitri and I attended different classes, we had quite diverse interests and soon enough both of us made friends among our classmates.

My first friend in London was Marion, she was a fourth year student who volunteered to help foreign students adapt to the language and customs.

The first year in London was incredible, learning to move around, seeing all of those fabulous and famous sites, palaces, and I grew to love the city.

We corresponded with our mother, and before the end of the year we asked her to come and visit us in England.

Dimitri offered to fly to Athens to bring her to London, and on the way back we would fly home all together. Mama was a modest woman, going out in the world was absolutely a challenge for her, but she said she would think about it… *'Maybe next year.'*

During that summer vacation in Pherula I continued my classes with the villagers, I had much more to tell them about what I had learned in England. Their eyes opened wide, I brought them books and pictures, and they couldn't believe how beautiful and majestic London was.

Their horizons were expanding, I felt gratified for being the one that could bring them that knowledge.

I told Father that I was determined to set up a school in the village. He didn't like that much, he said I would be wasting my time, and he had other plans for my future...

He was not in a good mood those days.

According to Mama she perceived that he was having problems with his business, which she knew nothing about, he would not share anything with her.

My brother and I thought we were weighing on him financially, and Dimitri spoke to Father. He said absolutely not and he gave us even more money, telling us that he was doing better than ever, the only issue was that some people were envious of his profits, but he would not quit!

None of us could understand exactly what was going on. To distract us and to prove that everything was well, he took us to a resort in the south of Evia, like he had done once during our childhood.

This time he brought the entire family! It was fun!

*'Just watch for the pirates!'* he would tell us.

We ended that summer... The aroma in the air, the sweet smell of the flowers and honey, the warm sea breeze, the colors of the water gently crashing down on the cliff.

Our home, our Greece, was so beautiful!

Mama accompanied us to Athens for our return to London. She told us that she had overheard Spiros and Father talking about issues and she was clearly concerned, she did not have a good feeling about it.

*'He was having a tirade! Something is not right with his business...'*

She promised to write us, which she did, telling us about our family, Pappous, who didn't leave the house anymore, the grandchildren growing up fast, the villagers' progress, but most of all how much she missed us and how she couldn't wait to see us on the next holiday.

Mama learned to make phone calls from Steni, she would make that trip just for a few minutes' call. I was so grateful to hear from her, it was sweet to hear her voice.

We were looking forward to our winter break, but our plan was changed. Before the end of that year Mama told us not to come to Pherula, the situation at home with Father was unusually tense. She clearly reiterated to us not to come until *'everything was resolved.'*

*'Everything what, Mama?'*

She did not explain.

Dimitri and I were terribly upset and worried, we asked her to come for the winter and stay with us.

*'It is quieter here, Mama, and we miss you so. Please come!'*

*'I miss you both much, but I can't go. Wait until we let you know when you should come home.'*

This all happened in the mid-seventies, we didn't have the same accessibility to communications as now, no social media, no internet.

In our village we didn't have electricity or phone lines, not even mail delivery. Our letters would take a long time to go back and forth. They were addressed to the Post Office in Steni, from there a driver of one of the trucks would pick them up and bring them to Pherula, and vice versa when our mother responded.

A month later we received a letter from Mama stating the same, *'Things were not right at home.'*

She asked us to remain patient and wait a little longer to go home after everything was in order. Still there was no explanation.

Dimitri was frustrated and felt compelled to go to Greece to verify what was happening. I begged him not to. *'Mama asked us to wait here, Dimitri!'*

Spring was approaching, and one day we got a call from one of the villagers in charge of the olive grove. He was calling us from Steni on behalf of our father, saying that he had serious business issues, people were threatening him and we should hide and not come to Pherula anytime soon.

The message was clear: *'Do not come now!'*

I was devastated and terribly upset, Dimitri almost ignored our father's recommendation and wanted to take a flight to Greece immediately. I urged him to wait for more information.

I was also terrified of being left alone in London, with my brother I always felt safe and secure, he took care of everything, made all decisions for us. I relied on him.

We were anxious, and about a week later the same man called Dimitri and told him bluntly:

*'Two days ago the frurio was attacked by smugglers from a rebel militia group, they took over everything, the house, your father's boat.*

*It hurts me to tell you... They killed your family, all of them, including the children, they are after every Pheris, they don't want any family member to claim the business!*

*I won't call again, I am afraid they will come after me. You and your sister should hide away, fast! They know of the two Pheris children in London.'*

We panicked! I was numb.

Dimitri desperately tried to call someone in Steni, hoping to learn more about what was happening. We were both confused and stunned, we didn't want to believe that our mother and our entire family were gone! And the children! We couldn't process it. It was harrowing!

Dimitri held me by my shoulders, shook me and told me we needed to leave London immediately.

*'They are in the frurio, they have our address here, they might have sent someone to finish us too... They are looking for both of us together, we better separate and hide elsewhere.'*

In the midst of my fog I remembered my friend Marion from school who left a semester earlier to return to her hometown of Cardiff, Wales, she had given me her address and insisted for me to come and spend time with her.

I told my brother I could go to Marion's in Cardiff for a while.

He agreed and thought it was a good idea.

*'Let's not waste time, pack only essentials, I'll take you to the train station.'*

He explained that I would go to Bristol and from there by ferry to Cardiff.

We left our flat in a hurry, in somber silence. I held on to my brother until we got to the train station, he bought me a ticket and divided all the money he had with me. I gave him Marion's home address and asked him where he was going.

*'I'm thinking I should go to Greece, this might not be true... Or I could go to my friend Emil's house in northern England, he had invited me, I'll write to you in Cardiff, then I will arrange a safe place for us to reunite soon. Don't worry, little sister, we will survive this!'*

He hugged me.

I felt terribly scared, and at that moment neither one of us could imagine the consequences of our hasty and immature decision.

*'I love you, Dimitri, we only have one another, take care of yourself and come to get me soon. Please, please, please don't go to Greece now!'*

Tears and more tears...

I told Dimitri I didn't want to go without him!

He didn't say anything else, just pushed me onto the train.

I boarded.

As the train started moving away from London, a feeling of desperation and doubt took over me, and I couldn't find a justification for what we had just done.

We were shattered, hurried, scared and inexperienced to foresee the consequences!

The unexpected and devastating news steered the course of our lives. From college students we became fugitives, running away from an invisible threat. Was that all real?

During the long trip the reality of what was happening hit me like lightning. Although my mind was clouded by the horror, I deeply regretted separating from Dimitri. We should have remained together until the end.

I wish I had a prescient sense of the consequences. I was a naïve and unprepared nineteen year old... Never had been alone or had ever made a decision on my own.

I had lost my entire family, I could not lose my brother, I didn't know how to live without him! I didn't want to live without him!

***

Sabrina read the first chapter of her mother's script over and over. She was devastated, in shock and horror, imagining her mother as an inexperienced young woman facing those disturbing events. It was heart-wrenching.

*'Dinora Pheris was Mom's birth name! How and why did she change it? Dimitri and Dinora, brother and sister, it makes sense.*

*Blythe, or better Dinora, was deeply connected to her mother and her brother, she loved them so. She and her brother made a huge mistake when they separated, those events shattered their lives...'*

Sabrina found her Mom's love of her homeland and her family deeply touching! 'Dinora' had a true communion with her village and her feelings of pure reverence for her land were visible.

She almost could hear her Mom's voice saying *'Riverenza,'* in her old style words that she used so often.

Sabrina had more unanswered questions.

'Was Mom lost in Wales? What happened to Dimitri? Did he go back to Greece? Was he killed too?'

The next few days she researched in her Mom's Greek books. She didn't find anything about Pherula, but saw many descriptions and pictures of sites in Evia described exactly like her mother had written...

She had a heart to heart conversation with Shelton, discussing her findings about her Mom's life in Greece.

"It is difficult for me to reconcile the idea of the girl she described as weak and dependent with the woman I know she was. Mom transformed her life and unleashed her strength and courage. She always had it in her, it took those devastating events to bring it to the surface.

My admiration for what my Mom did with her life after knowing what she went through has grown. How could she keep her earlier experiences and memories repressed for so long?"

"This is an incredible revelation for me too, Sabrina. She endured much emotional pain, now we know what caused her long term psychological trauma and dissociation from her past!

I wish she would have told me, I would have tried to comfort her on her devastating losses... Blythe lived with the emotional scars and buried troubled memories, silencing her longings for her lost loved ones and the place of her childhood..."

"There is more to be known, Shelton. I have many questions about how she lived in Wales, about my father. Why did she change her name? Paradoxical as it may be, it has become my mission to confront Mom's past.

Eventually I will continue reading, but right now I need an emotional pause, and besides, I am involved with a very difficult and demanding case at work. I can't take my attention away from it."

"Give yourself some time, Sabrina, these revelations are emotionally charged. We will discuss it further when you are ready, I am always available to you."

"I am glad I have you, Shelton, my father figure, Mom's true companion and love, and Robyn, she was like her sister, she is my second mother. We are united in this journey, we are 'Blythe's' legacy of love and true friendship, and together we are stronger!"

"Well said, Sabrina!"

Sabrina visited Robyn and described at length her Mom's early life in Greece. She concluded:

"Ma Robyn, more often than not, when we walked at the beach Mom would stop to contemplate the ocean, her eyes were lost on the horizon. I observed mostly on our outings along the coast when we encountered cliffs or rocky areas, particularly some spots on the Rhode Island coast, she would sit there for hours... Now I wonder if on those occasions she was remembering the views from her village, *'the magnificent views of the Aegean calm waters...'*

More than ever I am committed to bringing her back there. She refers to it as going back to 'Mother Earth's womb.' After researching, I did not find Pherula on any map. It's not an official village, it's a private property, like a farm or an orchard, and by the description of the location it might be terribly difficult to access."

"Now you know exactly where she wanted to be. I trust you'll figure out everything in time.

Bri, there is much you need to know before you bring her there, someday...

Protect your heart, darling, you are grieving and at the same time feeling pain for what your Mom went through. It is too much to bear.

In the meantime, come here to relax and sunbathe this summer, we are having some delightful days. Go out with Luciana, do not just work and be alone at home, thinking..."

"I will, Ma Robyn, I need to recover from many emotions. Luciana and her mother have been very supportive, Manuela brings me dinner almost every night, like you she is motherly. I am blessed to have you all in my life."

Many times, alone at home, Sabrina went to her mother's room, brought fresh flowers, sat on her bed and spoke...

"Mommy, I wish you could hear me, and I could hear you, thank you for sharing your history with me, the more I know the more I respect you, and I hurt for you.

The way you described your birthplace touched me, I promise I will bring you home, someday soon, I hope.

You are in my heart forever."

Finally, on a nice warm weekend Sabrina felt it was time to resume reading the next chapter.

She printed it out.

She let the cheerful sunlight in the room, made herself comfortable on the sofa, and began.

## CHAPTER THREE

# TWELVE YEARS IN WALES
## by Blythe Lisvane

*O*n the worst day of my life and with a heavy heart, I arrived at the port in the Bristol Channel and took an old cab to Marion's address in Cardiff.

To my disbelief no one was living there, the house was vacant. Desperately, I knocked at the next house's door, a lady came out and simply said:

"They moved away last month."

I felt I was going to collapse.

"Moved where? Did they leave an address?"

"All I know is they went to Aberystwyth, they didn't leave an address. We were not really friends."

"Is there anyone around here who was friends with them?"

"I don't know."

She closed the door in my face.

I sat on the front steps, numb!

'What do I do now? I need to call Dimitri, he is never going to find me.'

I was shaking and had no energy left in me.

A man was coming up the street, and I asked him about public phones. He directed me back to the closest train terminal.

Dragging my suitcase and a heavy backpack filled with books, I arrived at the station and went straight to the phone booths.

I was filled with anxiety and doubts. Confusing thoughts were running through my head. My mind was in total disarray, I couldn't think straight. But I made the first call to London, our flat. No answer.

Then I called the College, no one had seen Dimitri. They told me to call tomorrow...

'How am I going to find my brother? I don't know Emil's full name or where he is from... I should go back to London, but if I go *they* might get me too. Did Dimitri have time to run away? Or is he on his way to Greece?'

In total despair, I gave up and sat on a bench, grabbed my book bag over my lap, rested my head and sobbed uncontrollably like I never had cried before. All I wanted was to wake up from that nightmare or simply evaporate into thin air...

Someone touched my shoulder.

"Miss, do you need any help?"

I lifted my eyes, I couldn't speak.

The man sat next to me.

"I can see you are in distress, are you here alone? Is there anything I can do to help you?"

I told him, "I don't think anyone can help me, I just lost my entire family, I came to take refuge at a friend's home. She moved, nobody knows where to. I can't go back to London, my brother is lost too..."

"Be calm, please. You said you have a brother in London, did you try to call him?"

"I did, he is not there..."

"Let's try again, give me his phone number, or better, come with me to the phone booth."

I followed him, he tried to call our flat a few times, there was no answer. He tried the school's office, it was closed.

He spoke gently.

"What about the address of your friend here in Cardiff? I'll accompany you there, we might obtain some information."

I gave him Marion's address, he held my suitcase and we went on.

He was calm and reassured me that we would find a solution.

"By the way, my name is Byron Lisvane."

"I am Dinora, Dinora Pheris."

"I wish I had met you under better circumstances, Dinora. But believe me, everything will be alright."

He seemed kind and had gentle manners, and for no reason whatsoever I trusted him.


We went back to Marion's house, he did all the talking with several neighbors, and no one was able to give us any information. He suggested that we go back to the train station.

"I still have time to catch my train to Merthyr Tydfil."

He told me I needed to rest, I would find a solution the next morning with a clear head. He asked me if I wanted to go back to London or stay in a hotel in Cardiff. I was so deeply emotionally exhausted, I shrugged my shoulders, "I don't know."

"I can't leave you here alone, come with me, I'll take you home and tomorrow you will feel better."

At that moment I did not care about what was happening to me, a part of me had died that day. I couldn't think or foresee how much that compassionate man would become part of my life.

I followed him to his train…


I don't remember anything from that moment until we arrived at his house in Merthyr Tydfil.

I was in a total stupor and all of a sudden found myself standing in a room, while he was explaining to his wife Mildred why he brought me to their home.

"This girl just lost her entire family, she came to Cardiff to seek the help of a friend, but she has moved away. I couldn't leave her alone in this state at the train station. She is in shock, as we can see, it is just for tonight, tomorrow we will decide what to do.

Her name is Dinora, she has a brother in London, we will locate him."

Mildred held my hand and made me sit down. She brought me a glass of warm milk.

"Drink it, you'll feel better, we will keep you safe here."

I looked at her, not understanding how she could be so kind to someone she knew nothing about. She offered me her young daughter's room for the night. She brought me upstairs, fixed a bed, told me to rest and that in the morning I would feel much better and everything would be resolved.

They had two children, a boy Nathan and a girl Lydia, they were at the other side of the room, looking at me with curiosity.

The next day came around, and the next...

I lost track of time, I was paralyzed with anguish and pain, unable to articulate a logical word or make sense of my own thoughts and the situation I was in.

I didn't do anything but cry, mostly about being separated from my brother and knowing that I didn't have a family or a home to return to.

I lost myself in time, wishing just one thing: that I would die. I prayed for death to take me...

What seemed to be an arrangement for one night lasted months, during which I received attention and care from both Byron and Mildred. She practically force fed me and many times took me to the bathroom to bathe. They made it their mission to bring me back to life. They were equally compassionate and good hearted.

Byron was an iron salesman, he had worked in the local iron industry his entire life, and for the demands of his job he went to Cardiff often.

During his visits to Cardiff, while I was in his home, he returned to Marion's neighborhood to try to find a contact, to no avail.

He also called the College in London, leaving messages for my brother Dimitri, in case he would search for me there he would know where to find me.

Mildred started forcing me out of the bed into the living area to spend time with her children. She told Nathan and Lydia that I was a long lost relative recovering from an illness.

The children, nine and seven years old, were adorable, well behaved, they never asked me any questions. I started being affectionate towards them, like I was with my little nephews and nieces back in Pherula.

Oh, I could not think of my people or my village, the tears would start rolling down...

Through it all Byron assured me that my situation was only temporary. He and Mildred did everything they could to lift me up. I started having a sense of guilt for being a dead weight, and one day I gave them all the money I had.

"Please accept it, you have been feeding me and taking care of me, I do not want to be a burden."

That day, Byron told me that things were going to change, they were tired of seeing my self pity. He took me outside in the backyard to see the garden.

"Sunlight and fresh air will make you feel better. Dinora, you have to make an effort to accept reality and start living again. After the attempts I made to find your brother that resulted in nothing we have to conclude that he is probably gone. You need to move on and stop hiding, afraid that someone is going to come to kill you.

You were a college student, you should resume your studies and make a life for yourself."

At that point I had convinced myself that Dimitri was gone forever. I had lost hope of ever seeing him again.

"I have no place to go back to, my entire family has vanished, my life is over."

"It is not! Your new life is just beginning, right here with us. I had an idea that I shared with Mildred, and she thought I was foolish! Maybe, but think along, what do fugitives do to hide themselves? They get a new identity, a new name!

Listen up, Dinora, I have a plan. About a decade ago a cousin of mine and his entire family perished in an avalanche up north. They were never found.

My uncle, who was my father's older brother, succumbed after that tragedy, but before his death he left his lost family's papers with me to record the deaths officially, which I never did. I still have their documents.

Among them was a girl, Blythe Lisvane, she would be about your age now, and that is what I am offering to you, her identity, her name, for you to continue living here as part of our family, as a Welsh citizen, to go back to school, find a job.

We can't change what happened, but I can offer you a whole new future where you won't worry about being found and will forget about your tragic past."

"Why are you willing to do this for me, Byron? Isn't that illegal?"

"Because you are worthy, Dinora, you are too young and deserve a new chance in life, and if you keep it a secret, there'll be no trouble for either one of us."

"Blythe Lisvane! I'll have a new name and a new family, and the monsters that destroyed my family will never find me!

Thank you, Byron, you have been so caring, I am sure I wouldn't be alive without you."

That day I sensed that his feelings for me were more than just compassion, he was trying to rebuild my life, to protect me.

Looking back I realized that I was transferring to Byron the dependency and feelings of affection I had for my brother, conforming to his suggestions and ideas, allowing him to direct my life and make decisions for me. I clung to him.

I didn't know how to deal with fear and pain, I was emotionally dependent, to the point of being crippled and incapable of facing life on my own.

I discussed the issue of a new identity with Mildred, she was afraid that it could result in some legal consequences, but in her willingness to help me she was supportive. She made me promise that in becoming Blythe I would have to forget Dinora entirely and I would not talk or think about my Greek roots, and would never look back.

As a matter of fact both Mildred and Byron did not ask me questions about my family, the place I came from, on the contrary if I would say something they would stop me. Byron said that bringing up memories of my family would make me suffer unnecessarily and leaving all in the past would allow me to embrace the only option I had, a new life.

That is when my mental and psychological dissociation process started, I learned that not thinking or talking about my origin made me feel better, becoming emotionally detached from my heritage was an easier way to cope with my new reality.

Dysfunctional as it may be, it was easier to erase my past and start anew, and I accepted the idea of becoming a Welsh citizen with a clean slate. I was bound not to share the truth with anyone.

Little did I know that the truth would be buried in me but never forgotten. Eventually it would surface, causing me shame for betraying my true roots and my people, and feelings of self-condemnation damaged my self-esteem even further. I felt like a fraud.

Byron was a good man, and I believed he had the best intentions, but he did not have the insight that living in denial was not the way to resolve my problems.

I blindly submitted myself to his guidance. Ironically, that became the reason that broke us apart…

Many years later, life caught up with me, I matured, becoming self-reliant. My life lessons were ultimately learned.

I didn't make any friends outside Byron and Mildred's home. They constantly reminded me to 'stand still,' they meant 'don't think, don't talk.'

Before Byron took me to the local Department of Education, he instructed me that because I had no complete school records, I would have to declare that I had been home schooled and submit to all tests, to continue on to the next step.

"But, Byron, I don't speak the Welsh language, and I have an accent."

"Nothing to worry about! Wales is a bilingual country and English is the first language, all the tests are done in English.

Accent? We all have accents, local or regional. You can go back to college and start over right here. You would only lose the year you have completed in London."

I did everything he told me, and after one year of classes and tests and re-tests I obtained a certificate that put me back in college, right there in Merthyr Tydfil.

I didn't need to learn the country's language, but I did pick up some words with Mildred, she came from the north region where it was mostly spoken. It was my way of becoming more ingrained in the Welsh culture.

Despite my extraordinary metamorphosis and effort to erase my past, I kept the love for my Pheris family and my village sealed in a corner of my heart, and for all my life I quietly reminded myself that I was Adina's daughter and Dimitri's sister. But the pain of remembering them made me swiftly divert those thoughts and feelings, and I came to totally embrace my new persona. Dinora ceased to exist, she died along with the Pheris family...

During the next four years while I attended college, I continued living with my new family. The children accepted me as their cousin and I loved them, all of the Lisvanes! We did everything together, the only time I would go out alone was to school.

Mildred and Byron did not have a social life and rarely had friends over. They spent their free time on outings, as a family, which I was part of and learned to appreciate our city.

Merthyr, located in one of the most beautiful regions, was one of the largest cities in Wales, only twenty-three miles away from Cardiff. It was once the iron capital, and it depended economically on many iron industries.

Most of all it was rich in culture and wonderful scenery, and had many historical attractions.

There were plenty of outdoor activities, along mountain trails, downhill or climbing to Summit Centre. There were also numerous parks in tranquil settings and nature reserves. The people everywhere were warm and welcoming.

I developed a further interest in the Welsh culture, completing studies since its prehistoric origins, its etymology and history.

As a good citizen, I was enticed by the Welsh national identity, regarded as one of the modern Celtic nations. I also learned everything about the Industrial Revolution, the development of the mining and metallurgical industries that transformed the country from an agricultural society into an industrial one.

When I graduated from college, I took the advice of one of my professors and made my first important decision of moving to Cardiff alone to attend a grad program in anthropology.

The fact that I had an inherent passion for learning about people, cultures, places, and already knew Greek and had recently completed studies in Latin, steered me in that direction.

Byron and Mildred didn't want me to go, but ultimately, they told me they were proud of me for being able to move on.

Leaving my Lisvane family was also for an impassioned motive, I felt I needed to create some distance... With time my feelings for Byron had deepened, I had fallen in love with him and I was extremely conflicted, I couldn't betray Mildred's trust in me.

It was a crying fest when I left, Lydia, 'my young cousin,' had grown attached to me and made me promise I would come back to see her often. I did, every weekend, for a while.

In Cardiff I lived on campus, where I had the opportunity to make a little money working in the school laboratory.

Byron would come quite often on business but also to spend time with me, and together we enjoyed the lively city. With him, hand in hand, I came to appreciate Cardiff well, especially during the summer festivals that offered a profusion of dining experiences.

Cardiff was known as the city of castles, historic civic centers, it was also a green city and had a large arboretum in the heart of a city park.

We always had something new to do and explore, together.

Byron was very attentive, never left me alone, he made no effort in hiding his feelings and soon declared his love for me. He suggested we rent an apartment where we would be together. Although I was in a conflict of conscience, I came to accept his affection. In the warmth and security of his arms I would forget any doubts I had.

I moved into a lovely attic apartment, close to the University, that Byron rented and where he stayed with me often.

On those occasions, we felt like a happy married couple, like there was no one else in the world but the two of us.

To justify our relationship, Byron would remind me that I had seen with my own eyes that he and Mildred were not a loving couple, they were only friends.

There was an obvious coldness between them, I never witnessed them being affectionate with one another. But I loved Mildred, she was a wonderful friend to me, and I told him I would not want to hurt her. He did promise me that he would always honor his commitment to his family, he would never leave them. That made me feel at ease, knowing that I wouldn't be the cause for breaking up his family, and his children that he loved dearly would always have him in their lives.

In his honesty, some time later he did tell Mildred about the feelings we shared, she literally told him she didn't care if we had a relationship, but I should not come back to their house.

I was heartbroken for Mildred and the children. Even if I questioned myself and felt shame for the forbidden relationship, I did carry it on. For a long time I silenced my inner voice, I didn't have any closer friend than Byron, and I couldn't see my life without him. Our love affair went on for years.

Byron was my everything, my protector, my motivator, he was the love of my life.

During our time together I had the opportunity to accompany Byron on a few of his business trips and got to know other cities and regions of Wales. I was mostly impressed with the mountainous higher peaks in the north and central areas of the country.

It was a paradox that while maintaining a totally dependent, secretive relationship, I excelled professionally on my own, working and succeeding at the University, leading research studies and making a name for myself.

At one of the academic conferences in which I participated in Cardiff, I met a group of professors from the United States and among them, Robyn, from a renowned university in Boston.

We had common interests and started collaborating on a project from across the pond, a study on Celtic and British women that lasted for two years. While our professional and personal connection grew, she became my best American friend and in many ways a mentor.

During that period Robyn invited me to come to Boston, not only to visit but to join the University, permanently.

I thought that was an exciting proposition, but I wouldn't consider leaving behind the man I loved and the life I was accustomed to until the day that I had to make a decision, not considering my feelings or his!

I was surprised to find out I was pregnant, and nothing and no one was more important to me than the new life that I was gifted with.

As I realized the situation I was in, I couldn't give my child a half life, or a half truth, and right there I decided I needed to start over alone, away from Wales.

I told myself that when things don't go the way we expect, sometimes we have to leave it all behind and write a new script for our lives. I had done it before with Byron's full support. This time I felt confident I could do it on my own.

I didn't want Byron to influence my decision and I asked him for some time alone to reflect and plan. He knew I was offered a position in Boston, but he never thought I would consider it.

For the first time in my life, facing a serious, life-changing decision, I gathered my strength, and felt prepared to take on the sole responsibility of raising my child.

After twelve years, in considering leaving Wales, all came to clarity that although I was grateful for the opportunity and appreciated the beauty of the country, I never really bonded with it, it didn't become my true place, I did not belong there. At heart I was a Greek girl from an unknown village in a remote area…

In Wales I lived a borrowed life, with a borrowed family! And now I had high hopes that with my baby I would create an authentic life, in a new country, making it our own!

I phoned Robyn in the United States and accepted the offer, telling her that I was ready to move immediately. She started the paperwork necessary for my transfer. It took about three months to be completed.

I went to Merthyr Tydfil for the last time, armed with determination. I had mixed emotions, was anxious, scared about the future, but certain, absolutely certain, of what I was about to do.

I needed to say goodbye to Byron and I also wanted to sincerely apologize to Mildred. I couldn't leave without speaking to her, I had to tell her that through it all I always felt a sense of shame for the relationship I was nurturing with her husband, even if it was based on love, even if I never wanted him to leave her, I needed to confess that the love affair was wrong, it had to end.

I thanked her for all the years that she cared for me, I could never repay her.

I told her emphatically that I regretted the relationship Byron and I had, I never meant to hurt her or bring any hardship on her or her family. I did it out of love, but I didn't love only him, I loved them all!

To my surprise Mildred embraced me, she said she felt sorry for seeing me go, that she always knew that Byron loved me and our feelings for one another were true, but not possible. We were from two different generations, different worlds, most of all she always understood that when I accepted his affection I was emotionally vulnerable.

In her unselfishness Mildred offered to take care of my child, but with the condition that I would leave her with them, to be raised as their own. For a moment I imagined my baby being raised by that loving woman, having a brother and sister, a family...

She was generous and caring, I was humbled.

Byron was shocked and blindsided. He was devastated about not being able to help me raise our baby. He looked defeated.

I, on the other hand, felt a sense of liberation, in that moment I realized I was not only putting an end to our relationship, I was freeing myself from his power and influence, nonetheless I felt pain!

I could only compare the pain of leaving Byron to the one I felt losing my brother. It was one of the most difficult things I ever did, but it had to be that way. I told him that the new life I was carrying propelled me into being my own authentic self, and for that I needed to leave him and cut our ties.

I gathered my strength, all I could say in the end was that I loved all the Lisvanes, and my baby and I would always honor his family name.

He walked with me to the train station, and in our last embrace he said he respected my right to live my life the way I chose and that he was proud of me for being capable to follow my own path, but he begged me to write.

His last words were, *'I will love you and I'll think of you until the end of my days.'*

As the train started rolling I kept my eyes on Byron, standing on the platform, waving goodbye until he disappeared in the distance. I was hurting, I knew that was the last time I would ever see him, the last time I was in Merthyr Tydfil.

I left a twelve year life history in Wales, where from the day I arrived until the one I left, Byron was with me. Byron was my savior, my protector, my friend, my love.

I felt a mix of feelings, gratitude for the life he gave me, and relief for having resolved our situation that was a thorn of guilt in my soul.

That was the second time in my life that I left a loved one on a train platform to never see him again...

Twelve years before, I said goodbye to my beloved brother. For years I avoided thinking of him, it was too painful to remember.

That day I thought, 'What would Dimitri say if he knew what I am about to do? I am embarking on a new life to build my own little family, in another country, not depending on anyone. Would he be proud of me?'

At that moment the weight of having lost all my loved ones crushed my heart, but my spirit was strong, I felt lighter making the decision of leaving it all behind, not dwelling on my past.

There were many unknowns ahead for me. 'How is my life going to be in the United States? In Boston? Will I adapt to the new surroundings, people, circumstances?'

I remembered my mother's love for me and my brother, and her words: *'Families are stronger when they stay together, for better or for worse.'*

My heart was filled with love for the child I was carrying, I was not alone, with her and for her I had the courage to move away, focusing on the present and working towards our future.

I had my family, I could do anything!

\*\*\*

Sabrina put the papers aside, sobbing.

She was proud of her mother's courage and at the same time devastated for what she went through.

Luciana stopped by, like she did often.

"You are crying again, Bri!"

"I just finished reading my Mom's poignant story in Wales. At least I confirmed that my father loved her, they loved each other, but their love story seemed like a Greek tragedy, no happy ending. When she left with a broken heart, my father's last words to her were:

*'I will love you and I'll think of you until the end of my days.'*

That was her last entry, unfortunately Mom did not have time to continue writing... I wish I'd known more about her life there and about my father, I'm feeling that the only way to fill in the blanks is to do an inquiry, on location."

"Are you saying you are going to Wales?"

"Yes, since I started reading I decided to go to Wales first, then I'll proceed to England in an attempt to find my uncle or at least information on what happened to him."

"Sabrina, that is an awesome task, it might take a long time and effort."

"I need to do it, Luci. I won't be at peace with myself and I think my Mom won't either. She wanted me to know everything, I'll do this for her and for myself, then I'll bring her ashes to her resting place in Greece, as she wished."

"You are determined, I know how you feel, but don't make any rushed decisions."

"I won't, Luci. I have learned from what happened when my mother and her brother made an impetuous decision, they lost each other. I don't blame them, they were shattered."

It took a few days for Sabrina to get over the emotions she had been exposed to, reading her Mom's story. She was confused and had many questions, doubts, mostly about her father and their forbidden love connection. Was he really a good man? Unselfish?

Her curiosity about the Lisvane family only grew.

She wanted to share it with Shelton and ask his opinion, but he was out of town, at a conference.

By mid-week unexpectedly Tom called to invite her out. Sabrina thought she would never hear from him again, but she agreed in meeting him at a restaurant.

"I missed you, Sabrina, I am glad you have time for us. What have you been doing?"

"I have been invested in my Mom's past history, Tom. I still have a lot to figure out."

"Why do you need to investigate that further? You should be done with it."

"When my Mom's life ended a new life that I knew nothing about started for me. I need to know what happened, at least, I'll try."

"Forget about that, Sabrina! All you need is a little fun and you'll be alright."

"Tom, you can't understand me. What I needed from you was a word of support, I don't see any purpose in us continuing to discuss this matter."

"You need to relax, Sabrina. Do you want to go away like we did last year to the Bahamas?"

"No, Tom, I am planning a trip to Wales and England, probably in the fall, and then next year I'll be going to Greece to bring my

Mom's ashes."

"You are really obsessed with this, aren't you?"

"Obsessed? I feel a responsibility to honor my Mom's wishes."

"You are going too far, Sabrina. I have a suggestion, we can get a boat and spread her ashes in some rocky spot off the coast right here in the New England area. What's the difference?"

"I find it offensive. There is no point in discussing it with you. Why did you want to see me, Tom?"

"Well, we always had very good chemistry together. Why do we have to give that up? Maybe we can pick up where we left off, if you start acting like yourself again."

"Let me make it clear, Tom, I loved you and I overlooked many things but now I came to believe that you never loved me or supported me when I needed it the most. A true relationship does not survive on chemistry alone, therefore this is not what I want to invest my heart and my time in."

"Are you saying we are really done, Sabrina?"

"Honestly, we were done months ago, I can't deal with you now or ever, Tom! I am sure you'll find better company than me."

She walked out free, but feeling lonely. She put it all into perspective, she already had lost much more than a boyfriend and she was surviving.

Luciana, her constant and loyal friend, came over on a Sunday afternoon.

"I came to invite you for dinner. Mom prepared that Portuguese style cod that you like and told me to come and get you."

"You and your mother are such good friends. I am sorry, Luci, I have been consumed by all of this and I have totally neglected you. Whatever is going on in your life matters to me.

Please tell me, is everything with you and Jonathan alright? You haven't mentioned him lately."

"I have been anxious, so far our wedding plans haven't materialized for one reason or another, but finally after four years of dating, we are talking about getting engaged and set a date by the end of the year."

"That's good news, Luci, I'll be happy to help you with the preparations, wedding dress shopping…"

"I am counting on you, Bri. What about you, are you looking forward to meet someone new?"

"I have much more important matters to resolve now, but I didn't give up believing that someday I'll find my true, lasting love and soulmate!"

"You will, Bri. Let's go, time to eat!"

Manuela, Luci's mother, offered a savory meal accompanied by good Portuguese wine. For a few hours they talked, they laughed, and Sabrina had a delightful time with her caring friends. She ended that weekend on a good note.

The caring presence of her friends, Luciana, Manuela, Robyn and Shelton, has been an uplifting force throughout her time of mourning and searching.

Sabrina was determined to proceed in her discovery process, looking into her Mom's drawers and papers.

She located a safe box in the bottom of the closet. She had totally forgotten about it. It was unlocked, opening it up felt very invasive, but she knew she had her mother's consent to do so.

Inside there were two old passports, one Greek under the name of Dinora Pheris with a picture of a young seventeen year old. 'My Mom, so young, so pretty!' Another from Wales for Blythe Lisvane, the passport she used to come to America. And school records, one from the Imperial College in London, others from the Merthyr Tydfil Institute of Education and the University in Cardiff.

In the bottom of the box, she found a stack of letters tied up together, they were from Byron, post dated from the years 1987, the year her Mom left Wales, until 1991!

Her heart was racing.

'The records from London might help with the search for my uncle.'

Right then she decided she was going to write to the College asking for information. That gave her hope!

She looked around her mother's room, took all the contents of the safe with her, turned the light off and locked the door.

The next morning she drafted a letter to the College in London, asking for verification on the former Pheris students, thinking that perhaps they could find information about her uncle's whereabouts in 1975 in their files. It was a long shot, but that could be a start.

She mailed the letter that same day.

In the evening, alone at home, Sabrina held Byron's letters tight for a while. 'They came from my father's hands to my mother's, they both held these pages... This is a palpable piece of their history, their legacy to me. My parents.'

She decided to take her time reading one letter at a time, and that became her nightly routine.

The first one was a heartfelt acknowledgement that Blythe was perfectly installed in Boston and doing well in her last trimester of pregnancy. The entire letter was carved in poetic words of love. Through those lines she could almost feel his pain, how much he loved her, how much he missed her. There were also words of praise for Blythe's courage and determination, emphasizing how difficult it must been for her being alone without him.

In a letter after Sabrina was born, his words were filled with love and sorrow.

*'The child I would never hold in my arms but for always would be close to my heart...'*

He professed his undying love for Blythe and little Sabrina, *'our little princess.'* She also realized that for him she was not a forgotten child, he vowed his love for his daughter, even if he never saw or held her.

Sabrina read letter after letter, always talking about his undying love. It seemed like his intent was to maintain their connection, hoping that she would come back to him, as he stated often. In a few paragraphs he mentioned *'his heavy obligations and responsibilities'* that didn't allow him to come to be with *'his true love.'*

He wrote absolutely nothing about his family. That was puzzling!

Sabrina appreciated his simple but delightful style of writing. Like her mother he had a peculiar way of expressing himself, his words were emphatic and seemed heartfelt, but in the end she questioned his purpose.

'Was he really concerned about Mom living alone in another country or was he trying hard to lead her to return to him?

Why did his letters end in 1991? What happened? I need to find out. At least he proved he loved my Mom. He repeated over and over that he had a hole in his heart, longing for her...'

She spoke to Shelton.

"After reading about Mom's life in Wales and the letters from Byron, I don't have to make an effort to understand why Mom fell in love with him. He was her savior, her hero, the one who gave her a new life. He supported and guided her when she was alone and most vulnerable... But no matter what she wrote, that he was kind, generous, I have a feeling that she was manipulated...

What's your opinion, Shelton? You knew Mom so well, and with your professional expertise I trust your judgment."

"You are right, Sabrina, from a psychological point of view, I see the signs of abuse of power and control. She was just a girl when she met him in the most adverse time of her life, she was in shock, broken. He, an older man, took over her life, her destiny, out of the goodness of his heart or not, he crossed a line, he made her one of his own.

It is unheard of that someone would go to the extent of offering a new identity, under those circumstances. I'm sure you'll have a better insight once you meet him or his wife in Wales."

"I am distressed about this, Shelton, I don't attribute to Mom the responsibility for their relationship, I wish she had written more about it. She should not have carried feelings of guilt for that."

At work, Sabrina discussed her plans with Wyatt, her boss, who has been exceptionally understanding of her feelings lately.

"I am planning a trip to Europe to try to find my Mom's relatives. It's imperative that I do this, do you think I can take my vacations in late fall?"

"Sabrina, I understand what you are going through, and I appreciate the effort you have placed on your job responsibilities despite grieving. When you are done with the current assignment you may take two weeks off before we'll assign you the next case. Set the date and let me know."

"Thank you, Wyatt. I think I'll be done with this case by the end of October."

She scheduled her trip to Wales and London for November.

A response from the London College arrived three weeks later, informing her that they did not have old records available from ex-students who did not complete their courses.

Sabrina was frustrated, but still determined to press the issue when visiting London.

The next months went by very fast, she was extremely busy at work. At home she did more searches on Cardiff, Merthyr Tydfil and London, on names, addresses, anything that might help her.

She found out that Byron's return address was still under the Lisvane family name.

'They still live there!'

She got ready for the trip and spoke to Robyn and Shelton. They both supported her endeavor.

"You are brave, Sabrina, but it might be grueling, take good care of yourself, protect your heart and come back soon."

Sabrina said goodbye to Luciana.

"Please, Bri, do not disappear! Call, text, let me know where you are and how you are, I'll be thinking of you!"

During the flight to Wales, Sabrina was anxious in anticipation of meeting the Lisvane family.

'What if I knock on their door and they refuse to talk to me?'

She did not know what to expect…

## CHAPTER FOUR

# *FOLLOWING HER HEART*

*S*abrina arrived in Cardiff and went straight to Merthyr Tydfil, where she took a room in a central hotel.

The next morning, a dreary gray day, she was filled with anticipation, she went for a walk around the College that her mother had attended, to calm down.
She felt relaxed and decided not to call the Lisvane family in advance. She went to their home in a residential area on the outskirts of the town.

An older lady, probably in her late seventies, opened the door. Sabrina tried to keep her heartbeat under control and appeared calm.
"Good morning, I am looking for Mrs. Mildred Lisvane."
"I am Mildred. Who are you?"
"I am Sabrina, Blythe's daughter. Do you remember my mother?"

The lady, visibly shocked, held on to the doorframe, staring at her for a little while.

"Yes, I do, I can see the resemblance..."

"I am sorry I didn't call in advance, Mrs. Lisvane, I arrived from the United States last night and I would love to talk to you. Is this a convenient time? I'll come back later if you prefer."

"You may come in, Sabrina, I'd like to talk to you."

"Thank you, I hope I am not disturbing you."

"I am very surprised but not disturbed, as a matter of fact I wished your mother would have returned here. Why didn't she come with you?"

"My Mom died recently."

"I am sorry to hear that! Blythe was young, too young to die."

"Too soon and unexpected, and she left many unanswered questions about her life here in Wales. That's why I came."

"I am glad, I am alone and I have time to talk to you. I am curious, how did you find me?"

"I found some letters from Byron to my mother with this address. I didn't know of him until after she died, and reading the letters I realized that he stopped writing when I was about four years old."

"Yes, after Blythe left they corresponded for a few years."

"Do you know what happened, Mrs. Lisvane? I am afraid to ask, is your husband still here?"

"No, Byron died in 2001. The reason he stopped writing was because Blythe put an end to it."

"I don't know what to say, I am sorry. I had hoped that he would still be here... I would have loved to meet him and know more about him."

"It is alright, he is gone for a long time now. But before we start, would you like to have some tea with me?"

"I would love to, thank you, Mrs. Lisvane."

Mildred went to the kitchen and brought tea and biscuits, they sat comfortably, and she started:

"First, I will tell you about their letters. In 1991 Blythe wrote to him, one last time, terminating their communication.

I did read it, she said you were in pre-school and started asking questions 'about Daddy.' You wanted to know where he was, when he was going to come, she didn't want to tell you lies and she wouldn't tell you the truth about him, either.

She said she was totally independent in her new life, and the letters were feeding their severed emotional connection, which was conflicting. In order to be true to herself she broke away from binding ties with him, and there was no reason to maintain their communication.

Blythe did tell him the only thing she would tell her daughter was that he was a good man and she loved him.

Bluntly, she said a final goodbye and asked him never to contact her again!"

"How did he take it? Was he upset?"

"He was devastated, the letters were the only thing he had to nurture their connection. From then on Byron became somber and bitter.

Throughout the years he still wrote her many love letters, but never mailed them... I found them after he was gone."

"My heart breaks for him, also for you who had to see all of that happening. Did you keep any of the letters Mom wrote to him? I am curious about what she wrote."

"I did not, but I read them and destroyed them all after he died. It was clear that her feelings for him had changed, they were not love letters, they were basically informative, talking about her career successes and challenges, about you growing up, and in every letter she always mentioned me and the children with affection."

"Mom had true affection for all of you. Would you like to tell me more about him?"

"Byron was a compassionate and good-hearted man, father and friend, he left a legacy of good deeds to many. One of them was to offer shelter to your mother in our home, without even knowing her.

Right here in this same room I saw her for the first time, she looked frightened, like a little bird caught up in a windstorm. I felt sorry for her. She was too young, alone, broken. For months she didn't do anything but cry for her family, for her lost brother."

"Did she say anything that could be a possible lead to him? I am also looking forward to find my uncle."

"No, nothing. After a while Blythe came to accept that he was dead. Didn't she find out what happened to him?"

"No, she didn't, but I am looking for a resolution, one way or another, I am going to London after I leave here."

"It's always better to have closure! But going back to Blythe, we helped her starting a new life. Do you see? This is not a big house, but we shared with her what we had."

"Mrs. Lisvane, my mother left me, in writing, how much care and friendship she received from you. She was very grateful. I'm sorry to bring the past back but I need to ask you, did she cause any damage? Did you ever separate from your husband?"

"Byron and I never separated, we remained friends through it all. Our marriage had been promoted by our families, like most of the marriages of our time, I loved him, but we were never in love.

Since the beginning I could see that he was very attracted to Blythe, he was fascinated by her manners, by her beauty. She was very dependent, relying on him for everything, until years later when she moved to Cardiff, that's when their romantic relationship started.

Honestly, I was hurt and disappointed. I told him that I didn't want her in my house anymore. I didn't want my family to be broken and our children to suspect what was going on. Until then she used to come often to visit, my son and daughter enjoyed her company very much.

Byron promised me he would never leave us, but he continued seeing her and spending a great amount of time in Cardiff with her.

I didn't see her for years until she came to tell us she was moving to America and about the baby she was going to have...

In that moment, the only thing I could think, because it was Byron's child, was to offer her to leave the baby here with us. I would have raised you! Blythe was humble, she thanked me and apologized. I believed her, she was sincere and I felt truly sorry to see her go, she was like family to me, and again, there she was, going away alone to a foreign land. I admired her courage.

Byron was devastated, hurt, he did try to dissuade her, but there was nothing he could do or say that would make her change her mind."

"Mrs. Lisvane, I find it admirable that you didn't harbor any hard feelings towards her. My Mom was a wonderful person, she admitted that she betrayed your trust and carried a great amount of guilt and regret."

"I am sorry she did, I never blamed her. I knew it was true love at least from Byron's side, he never loved any woman like he loved her. For Blythe he was everything, her best friend, her protector, she looked up to him, they would go on talking for hours when he bathed her with his charm. Oh, he was charming and she was just a girl..."

"You are an exceptional human being, Mrs. Lisvane, and I thank you for recognizing my Mom's feelings. May I ask you, what motivated you to help a complete stranger, taking her into your home as part of your family?"

"I supported Byron's decision, he was persuasive, I must say. And I felt so sorry for that young girl, lonely and devastated, not wanting to live. I made it my mission to lift her up."

"It was an admirable act of kindness and generosity from your part, Mrs. Lisvane. What do you mean about him being persuasive?"

"I don't want to speak badly of him, but I think you deserve the truth. That's what you are here for, isn't it?

Byron had many qualities, no doubt, but he used his power and skills to persuade people to fulfill his own interests, 'sweet persuasion,' as I called it."

"Please, could you tell me more, Mrs. Lisvane?"

"For instance, when he hatched a plan to give Blythe a new identity, I thought it was an outrageous solution, I believed that in the predicament she was in, hardly functioning, she was not apt to make any important decision regarding her future. I suggested he take her to London to search for her brother. He dismissed it and convinced me that the best solution was to keep her as part of our family. According to his words it was 'all in the name of love for another human being with no one left in this world.'

He also told me to discourage any conversations that Blythe might have about her family or the place she came from, he said that those memories would hurt her.

I didn't quite agree but at that time my life was uneventful, only taking care of the family, the house, helping someone in need gave me a purpose."

"You are really exceptional, Mrs. Lisvane. But, sorry to say, it seems to me he was manipulating you and her."

"Took me a long time to admit it, but now I can say I agree. Byron's gentleness disguised his ulterior motives. That skill made him a superb salesman."

"Thank you for this explanation and for understanding the difficult situation my Mom was in.

May I ask you, did your son and daughter know of their romantic connection?"

"No, they never knew of their father's relationship or of another child, and I didn't want them to ever find out. They revere the memory of their father until this day. Nathan and Lydia still miss him.

In all fairness he was a caring father, that's the main reason I stayed with him until the end."

"In that case, they do not know I exist?"

"They don't, I am sorry. They are your half brother and sister, but this is a secret I want to keep to preserve Byron's memory."

"I understand. Right now I am having an identity crisis, I have a borrowed name, I am an illegitimate child.

Do you have any feelings about me carrying your family's name?"

"Our name fits you well, Sabrina, you are a fine young woman, and Byron would have been happy to meet you and embrace you."

"I would have been too, I always longed for my father, my Mom was an exceptional mother but I missed not having a father."

"It's not fair that you didn't have that experience. Didn't Blythe ever marry?"

"No, she didn't want to get married. When I was ten years old she started a relationship with a fellow professor that lasted until she died. I love him, he is still my friend and the only father figure I had.

Mrs. Lisvane, I see you have those picture frames on the wall. May I see them up close? Would it be too much if I asked you for a photo of him?"

Mildred got up and started describing the family pictures, pointing out her son and daughter at different ages and the newer ones of her grandchildren, five of them.

"This is our Byron, my husband and your father. Look how handsome he was! You have his eye color, just like my daughter's, 'the color of the ocean.'

You don't need to ask me, Sabrina, you are his child, and I'll give you a picture for you to remember the face of a kind, generous man who never held you but loved you."

"I truly appreciate it, Mrs. Lisvane. Would you mind telling me where he is buried? I'd like to visit before I go away."

"I would come with you if I could, I don't go out much anymore. But, you should go, Sabrina, it is not far from here."

She wrote the directions down on a piece of paper.

"I feel emotional, I imagine my mother receiving your attention and love, and then that happened... I can see why she wouldn't tell me the truth, my mother was a good woman, a good human being, she never meant to hurt you, I am sure. I am glad you forgave her long ago, maybe she never forgave herself."

Mildred came closer.

"Give me a hug, Byron's daughter, you too are part of him! I hope I gave you the peace you deserve, you are an innocent child."

"You did and more, you enlightened me! You are an amazing person, I am so glad I came to see you, Mrs. Lisvane. Thank you for allowing me into your home. Thank you for helping my Mom when she needed it the most. She did love you, never forgot you, I'll never forget you!"

Sabrina left feeling she had just met an extraordinary human being in that modest home. She had a knot in her throat, but didn't break into tears in front of Mildred. That compassionate woman made a significant impression on her and brought her clarity.

She confirmed her father was a good but misguided man, and she felt sorry she would never meet her half brother and sister. She saw them in the pictures, but would never talk to or hear from them. Would they be like their mother or their father? Would she have anything in common with them? Ironically, she had some family in this world, after all.

She walked around the town for a while, tracing her Mom's footsteps, bought a bouquet of flowers, and stopped at the cemetery.

It was easy to find the family tomb where she saw his name

engraved:

Byron Nathan Lisvane – 1939 – 2001.

Her first thought was, 'They both had a lot of life to live, he was sixty-two and my mother died at age sixty!'

"Today I came here to call you Father, I wish I had known you, I wish I had received the warmth of your love, if circumstances had allowed. My Mom loved you, she was thankful for your good deeds and forgave your weakness, and I forgive you too.

My Father, I'll keep you in my heart, praying that you are in peace."

She sat there for a while, not wanting to go away, feeling that was the only opportunity she would have to be close to him. She looked at his picture. 'I'll remember you, charming, handsome, smiling...'

Later she went to the hotel feeling the trip was all worth it, she obtained the information she needed and meeting Mildred brought her closure. She picked up her luggage and took a train back to Cardiff.

The next morning she walked through the city, like she did in Merthyr, then took a ferry to Bristol and proceeded to London.

The same melancholic journey her mother had taken decades before…

She arrived in London, found a hotel not far from Victoria Station on Buckingham Palace Road, and planned that the first thing she would do the next day would be to go to the College to try to find any information about her uncle.

At the College's office, using her best attorney skills she pleaded to some people. Initially they said they couldn't help her, but after her insistence they directed her to the administrator.

"You sent me this letter informing me that there were no records available, but I flew all the way here because this is a most important family matter. Please, is there any way of finding those records?"

She made a compelling case and also mentioned the name Emil. "I don't know his last name, he was probably a classmate of Demetrius Pheris, my uncle."

The administrator heard her attentively and expressed some sympathy.

"I understand the reasons you need to find your uncle, I need to explain that the records of our students are always private, but in a case like this I'll give it my best consideration. I can't make any promises, you need to sign a formal request and I'll get an approval from the Dean to proceed.

Anyway the records from the seventies were not computerized, they were placed in the archives. Please contact me in two days."

"I truly appreciate your attention to this matter, I'm hopeful!"

During those two days Sabrina decided to personally research in the areas of London populated by Greek nationals: Soho, Camden, Palmers Green, Chelsea.

She had a long list. She started in Soho and went street by street to every restaurant and other businesses, asking people if they had known Demetrius or Dimitri Pheris and his sister Dinora.

During two exhausting and frustrating days she didn't obtain any results. Some people asked if she had a photo of them, others remarked that half of Greek men are called Dimitri or Demetrius… It would be almost impossible to find him.

On the third day Sabrina called the administrator, who told her she had the information available.

She went to the College immediately.

The lady had two old files on her desk.

"I will give them to you, in my presence you may look through them carefully and take notes, but you can't remove anything, the registrar will make copies if you need."

"Thank you!"

Her heart was racing. She had both academic records of her mother and uncle in her hands.

Excited, she looked in the files and shockingly found notes in both of them with their phone numbers to find one another in case they called the school. She told the registrar:

"Look, they both left an address to be located, but it was misplaced! If someone looked in Dimitri's file all they would see were his own notes about his whereabouts, and vice versa!"

The administrator looked at the files.

"You are right! How unfortunate! Sadly it fell through the cracks..."

Sabrina was shaking, in his file there was a handwritten note:

'In the event that my sister Dinora tries to locate me please inform her I am at Emil Vorta's home, 6444 Fleet Road, Leeds, U.K. Phone 55-11-44-9999.'

In Dinora's file, there was one note, a record of a phone call from Byron confirming the address where she could be located in Merthyr Tydfil...

The registrar made copies of all the papers for Sabrina, including their application pictures. For the first time she saw a picture of a young Dimitri, brother and sister looked pretty much alike. There was also the address where they used to live in South Kensington.

Sabrina's heart was broken, she couldn't contain her tears and told the administrator:

"They could have found each other if these papers weren't misplaced... But from the bottom of my heart I thank you for your interest in helping me."

As she was leaving the College she realized it was very close to their former residential address, she went straight there.

It was a fine street of townhomes. She found three door bells, rang the first one, assuming that each one of them was for one of the apartments, flats, as they are called.

The ground floor lady opened her door, and Sabrina asked her where she could find the landlord.

"I am the landlady, if you are looking for a flat I have no availability."

"I am not, thank you. I don't believe you are old enough to have been here in the seventies when one of these flats was rented to a brother and sister from Greece, I suppose!"

"I grew up here, I was a child then, my mother was the landlady. How can I help you?"

"That brother and sister were my mother and my uncle. My mother died recently, and I am looking for my uncle or anything that may lead me to him."

"You won't believe it, but I remember them. My mother was terribly upset when they suddenly disappeared, she packed and kept some of their things that she considered valuable, like books, photographs... Years later the man came back."

"Was he here? Did you see him?"

"Yes, I remember he was a handsome lad... He came to ask if anyone or his sister had looked for him. Unfortunately, we never saw his sister, but my mother gave him the box with the belongings.

He was very grateful and left a phone number in case his sister would come looking for him someday."

"Oh, that's good news! Do you have that phone number?"

"I am sorry, no. Since then my mother has passed, I don't know what she did with it, we are talking more than thirty years ago..."

"Thank you for the information, at least I know he was here, I want to believe that he is still in England."


Feeling encouraged she took a cab back to her hotel and tried the old number for Emil in Leeds.

The woman's voice at the other side said that was still the family residence, but Emil had died about four years ago.

"I am sorry to hear that, I was looking forward to ask him about one of his friends, Demetrius or Dimitri Pheris."

"I don't know his old friends, but you can call later and talk to Chester, my husband and Emil's son, he might know."

"I thank you very much, please tell him I am a relative of the Pheris family and I am trying to contact my uncle. I will call later."


Sabrina anxiously waited a few hours and called again. This time she spoke to Chester.

"My father had a friend called Dimitri, but his last name was not Pheris."

"Sometimes people are known by other names... Anyway does

that Dimitri live in Leeds? Do you have a phone number for him, please?"

"He lived here for a while, but he moved to Manchester. The last time I saw him was when he came to my father's funeral, years ago. No, I do not have his phone number."

"Sir, forgive me for insisting, it is so important to find my uncle. Do you know of anyone else that would have any contact with him? A common friend, maybe?"

"I know that Dimitri was married to a lady who was my aunt's friend, I will ask her. Call me back tomorrow at this same time."

"Absolutely, I appreciate your help."

Sabrina hung up the phone feeling optimistic! She didn't go out for dinner, she laid on the bed and fell asleep, exhausted from the eventful day.

The next morning, famished, she had breakfast at the Hotel and started thinking about what she was going to do until the afternoon.

'Enough of reading the entire phone book and walking and asking door to door for information.'

She decided to take a look around the area of Buckingham Palace Road, Victoria Station, went all the way to Westminster Abbey and returned slowly, her feet were killing her after so much walking over the past days... But at every step, led by pure intuition, she felt her search was coming to an end.

Back at the Hotel she called Chester in Leeds, and he gave her a phone number in Manchester.

"My Aunt Rissa is friends with Layla Thanov, Dimitri's wife, and this is her home phone number, you may call her. Good luck on your search."

Sabrina's heart sang!

'I have his phone number. I found him, I am sure I found my Uncle Dimitri!'

She decided not to call and researched online first. Manchester, family name Thanov, restaurant! And bingo! She found two restaurants and a third one inaugurated about three years ago in London by Victoria Station!

'Is this a coincidence or what? I might have walked by it this morning...'

Oh, the thrill of discovery!

She couldn't explain that tingling feeling, but felt that she was very close to finding her uncle. She felt like running to the restaurant. It was too early for dinner, but she went anyway, walking slowly and doing some controlled breathing. She remained hopeful but cautious, she couldn't afford to be disappointed.

She arrived at the restaurant and a friendly maître'd offered a small table in a corner, which she appreciated. As she looked to her left she saw a picture hanging on the opposite wall that gave her chills.

It was a painting of a magnificent view of a rocky cliff, not too tall, with the water crashing down, on top of the cliff was a construction of boulders and rocks, she felt she had heard about that view before, in her mother's story...

*'Astoundingly, from spring to fall, the cliff wall facing the sea looked like an everlasting suspended garden of lush blooming bushes growing out of crevices in the rocks. A breathtaking view!'*

She was shaking. "Breathtaking," she whispered.

The maître'd standing close by observed her reaction to the painting and commented, "Beautiful, isn't it?"

"Yes, beautiful! Where did you get it? Where is it from?"

"It is a place in Greece, my father had it painted especially for our restaurants."

"Excuse me for asking you, is your father's name Demetrius or Dimitri Pheris?"

"My father is Dimitri, like half of the men of Greek origin, but that is not our family name. Are you alright, Miss? I see that you are a little shaky, I'll bring you some water."

He came back with water and served her. She couldn't stop looking at the picture and spoke to him.

"I know you have a job to do, and I also do not want to give you the wrong impression, I am not flirting with you, but when you have some time I'd like to talk to you."

"I have time, I am my own manager. I'll come back in a while after attending to some other customers. In the meantime I'll send you a waiter for your order."

The waiter came, she asked for the house special.

She ate slowly, savoring each bite while staring at the picture.

'That's Pherula, the frurio, the plateau... I am sure!'

The gut feeling and emotion running through her body told her so. She also felt like her mother was right there with her, smiling.

That painting was the key, it was a sign!

A little later he came back, she asked him to sit down.

"My name is Maurice, I can see you are American, Miss..."

"I am Sabrina, yes, I am American, from Boston. I came here to find a long lost relative, my uncle. My mother died recently and if I find him he would be the only relative I have left."

"I understand how important it is to find a family member, is there anything I can help you with?"

"That picture on the wall reminds me of a description that my Mom gave me of her birthplace on the island of Evia in Greece, your father might know where it came from. Would you please ask him if he knew a Demetrius Pheris and or his sister Dinora? They were always together!"

"I'll ask him, certainly. Dad lives in Manchester, I'll phone him."

"Without imposing, would you please call him tonight? I have a feeling he knew them. Please tell him I am Dinora's only daughter!"

"I will, where are you staying, Sabrina? I'll call you with his answer."

"I am staying at the Ruben Hotel, not far from here at all."

She gave him the phone number for the Hotel.

She left sensing a certain familiarity with Maurice.

'He is Dimitri's son... This strange feeling is not only wishful thinking, I know it!'

Maurice called her early the next morning.

"I spoke to my father last night, and he is going to help you locate your uncle, he is coming to London today. Would you please stop by the restaurant this afternoon?"

She couldn't stop smiling all morning, a sense of relief and certainty descended upon her. She prayed:
'Mom, stay with me, I am doing this for you, I am meeting your beloved brother. Oh, I miss you so! I wish you were here to share this moment!'

In the corner of her heart there was a little twinge of pain thinking that this could have happened if her mother believed her brother was alive, and if she had told her daughter sooner. Blythe, or Dinora, would have departed from this life with a sense of closure. It was sad that all that time was wasted!

She went to the restaurant around 3:00 pm, walking, trying to control her heartbeat, fast with anticipation...

Maurice greeted her and accompanied her to the back office.
"You'll have more privacy to talk there, my father is waiting for you."
He opened the door, she saw an energetic older man with gray hair and a big smile, he looked familiar.
He approached her, his eyes were watery, he didn't say a word and gave her a picture of a girl and a young man smiling, standing by the front gate of the College, the same one she had just visited a few days ago...
She took the picture, her eyes welled up.
"This is my Mom when she was young, so young. And this... this is you! You are my Mom's brother!"
"Sabrina, Dinora's daughter, I am your Uncle Dimitri!"

They embraced, a long embrace, with many tears rolling down their faces. They couldn't speak. Maurice, watching them, was teary too.
"Hey, I am your cousin, give me a hug!"
Then he left them alone.

Dimitri spoke first.

"Last night when Maurice told me about you, I cried first for knowing that my beloved sister was really gone, then finding out that she left a daughter, I couldn't wait to meet you, Sabrina.

You look like Dinora, even the little dimples! You are beautiful and I bet smart like she was. She was the smartest of us all. I want to know everything about her life, about your life."

"We do have much to talk about, so much, I also have many questions. In this moment I feel like my Mom is smiling in Heaven at us. She is the one who guided me here. I am sorry I didn't know about you until after she was gone... I would have found you to give her this joy on earth."

"I always think of her... I used to call my sister Nora, and I named my only daughter Norah after her. Dinora called me Dim, start by calling me Uncle Dim.

Sabrina, you are my newest daughter! Until now I had three children, today I have four!"

"Thank you, Uncle Dim, I welcome you in my life, I never had a father, and I also want to know everything about your life, your family, my cousins..."

"I was young when I married Layla, by age twenty-five I was already a father. We had Cassius, he is thirty-eight now, then came Norah, thirty-four, and Maurice is thirty-two. You look younger than my children, how old are you?"

"I am twenty-eight, it was the saddest birthday of my life without my Mom..."

"No more sadness, Sabrina, from now on your life will be filled with joy with your new family, you'll never be alone."

They continued the conversation. Dimitri told her about his struggle and desperation to find his sister.

"I sent many letters to Cardiff, most of them were returned. As time went by I came to believe that I had lost my sister forever. I regretted to the depth of my soul separating from her. It was the worst mistake I ever made."

"She felt the same way and she tried to find you too, she left a phone number and address where she could be located, at the school."

"I called the Police in Cardiff to report a missing person, they could do nothing, they weren't sure she even got there. I called our

College and left information on my whereabouts. Years later I came back to London and went to the school, asking them to verify our files. They said there was no information about Dinora."

"Uncle Dim, coming here now, I requested your files and found out there was some misplacement, both of you had left contact information but they were never given to either one of you... They had them all along."

"My heart hurts for Dinora! It's painful to think that we could have found each other. After a while I stopped looking, I believed she was gone."

"She did too, that's why she stayed in Wales and never returned to England."

"How was her life in Wales, did she finish college there?"

"Yes, you would be proud of her. Mom lived in Wales for twelve years until she went to America as an anthropology professor... I have much to tell you about her achievements."

Sabrina told him of her recent visit to Wales to see where her mother had lived and started her professional life.

Maurice brought them dinner in the office.
"It is dinnertime, here is more private."

Hours went by, they couldn't stop talking. Maurice came back.
"It's late, we closed the restaurant, do you want to come back with us to my apartment, my wife will love to meet you!"

"Thank you, Maurice, I think it is better if I return to the Hotel, I have my things there..."

"And I invited Sabrina to come with me to Manchester tomorrow, we will have a family reunion to meet everyone this weekend," Dimitri told his son.

They drove her to the Hotel.
Dimitri would be back in the morning to take her to Manchester by train.

During the train trip Dimitri told her that after he had separated from Dinora and arrived in Leeds with his friend Emil, he met Layla, a friend of Rissa, Emil's sister.

Layla supported him through the trauma he was suffering. He went to work with her father in the food business.

They fell in love and two years later they were married. Layla's family was originally from Bulgaria, and in their culture a man without a family, entering another's, had the opportunity to adopt his wife's family name. Her family practically adopted him. His father-in-law helped them open their own restaurant, and years later, they settled in Manchester.

"That is what I did. It was my way of hiding my name and coming out into the world, until then I was still afraid of being found. I hated my father's name then, he was the one who caused the destruction of our family."

"Do you know exactly what happened in the village?"

"I do, but I don't like to talk about it. Decades ago I hired an investigator in Athens who gave me a full report. I have it at home, do you want to read it?"

"I understand you don't want to talk about it. Yes, I would like to read it."

"Of course, Sabrina. You said you have writings from your mother too, can I see them?"

"Yes, she had many writings published about her studies, she was well known. But the most important paper is the one that she was desperately writing before the end. It is the story of your lives."

"Would you read it for me? Dinora always read out loud for everyone. It's a great memory that I have of her, and I hear her in your voice..."

"I will, Uncle Dim, I will."


She told him her mother had also changed her name, but the circumstances were quite different due to Byron's advice.

"That was not like Dinora, it was not only a name change, she eradicated her Greek origin... But I can understand the influence she was under then. What about your name? Where did you get it from?"

"Mom always told me that Sabrina was a legendary princess, but I came to learn that the princess was the illegitimate child of a British king. Isn't that suitable for me?"

"No! It's a beautiful name, and you are the legitimate daughter of a wonderful woman!"

Their arrival in Manchester was well celebrated.
Cassius was waiting for them at the station and greeted Sabrina
with much affection. "Welcome home, American cousin!"

At their large and comfortable home, Layla welcomed her with
open arms.
"Come, you are one of us, you are the missing link that Dim
cried for all these years, it is like his sister finally came home."
She brought Sabrina to a guest room.

Later she came back downstairs. Soon Cassius' wife Fiona
joined them with their three children: two girls, Shirley and
Audrey, and a little boy Jeremy.
Sabrina was impressed with Cassius, he looked and sounded
just like his father. She noticed that none of them had Greek
names, not her cousins nor their children.
"Norah will come tomorrow, she is out of town on business.
Prepare yourself, my daughter looks pretty much like my sister.
She is single, she'll love to have a younger cousin, she was
disappointed when Maurice was born, she really wanted a little
sister."

In the evening, after the festive dinner, Dimitri gave her the
report about Pherula.
"This is your copy. Read it when you feel like it."

The next day, sitting outside on the porch facing their beautiful
backyard garden under the morning sun, he asked her to read
Dinora's writings. She brought the printout, sat beside him and
started:

*'I was born in a remote area of Evia, the second largest island
in Greece...'*

During the reading Dimitri shed a few tears.
"Listening to Dinora's words, I could see us growing up among
the rocks and flowers, and I could feel our mother's presence. She

was vibrant and young, she was our best friend, and in your voice I hear my sister's. May I ask you, Sabrina, did you bury her in Boston?"

"No, Mom asked me in her will to take her home, to Greece... After I read this I was quite sure that she wanted to go back to the village."

"Your mother always wanted to go back, she had plans of establishing a school and teaching everyone, she loved the island and the people. Yes, she wanted to be there. Where are you keeping her ashes?"

"At home, in her room. What about you, Uncle Dim, did you want to go back to Greece? Why didn't you claim your property?"

"After you read the report you'll know that the grove belongs to the villagers, it is their livelihood, they have worked very hard for it, generation after generation. For me going back would have been too painful.

But I miss it and right now I am motivated to go with you to bring Dinora's ashes. I'll do it for my sister and you.

It's decided, we will go together!"

"Thank you, I'd love to have your company and support, Uncle Dim, it will be very difficult for me to let go of my Mom to her final resting place..."

"You'll never let her go, she lives in you."

Norah joined them in the afternoon.

Sabrina became very emotional, "You look so much like my Mom, it is like having her back, young, pretty, healthy!"

"And I love meeting you, Sabrina, I'll be like a big sister to you, I always wanted a little sister..."

Those two newfound cousins established a good relationship, like they had been together for years.

Norah told her of her amazement in finding her father had a niece he never knew existed. Being a partner with a graphic design internet company she was the first to say:

"If my father and his sister had grown up in our time of broad social media and internet access, they would never have lost contact. It is sad to think how something that is so trivial to us would have changed the course of their lives..."

"I agree and I feel sorry, before I started my search I didn't realize how easy it was for people to lose contact, mostly when they had to rely on others to maintain communication."

Norah also shared personal and professional aspects of her life. She told Sabrina that years ago she moved to London with two other friends to establish their company, one of those partners was her fiancé, but the wedding never happened... He left her and the partnership, she was broken financially and emotionally, and her parents were of great support to her.

"My Dad came often to help me and nurture me, and here I am, strong and successful. You won't miss anything if you accept my Dad's love and support, he is the best!"

"I know he is, my Mom wrote all about him, and I feel so lucky for having found him. It was fate! Destiny!"

On Sunday everyone was there, Maurice came with his young wife Daphne and their eight month old baby boy.

For the first time Sabrina observed her entire new family together: uncle, aunt, cousins, their spouses, and the children calling her 'Aunt.' She never had an experience like that before, a warm feeling of belonging.

Layla came to her, "This is your family, we are all here for you, Sabrina. You will never be alone!"

And the time to return home arrived. She told Dimitri and Layla she needed to go back home to her job, "Otherwise I am going to lose it."

"We don't like to see you going, but we understand you have an important job and you still have a long time ahead to build a career, but we would love to see you soon. Would you be able to come back for the holidays? This year we will celebrate you!"

"I would love to, but the end of the year is very busy for me, I can't come back this soon."

Dimitri told her, "In that case I'll come to visit you in Boston, I want to see where my sister lived all of these years, her home, her books, and spend some time with you, my niece, to plan our trip to Greece."

"I would love that, Uncle Dim. In the meantime we will talk!"

Dimitri and Layla brought her to the airport in London.
She hugged both of them.
Her uncle told her, "I feel connected to my sister again, you are the link!"
"Thank you for all the love, I'll never let go of you, my family! I won't say goodbye, I'll see you soon!"

She boarded the airplane with a heart filled with new emotions! She rested all the way to Boston.
Emotions are exhausting!

## CHAPTER FIVE

# BACK IN BOSTON

*R*eturning home, overwhelmed by the deeply emotional experience, Sabrina needed to recover from an array of mixed feelings of sadness and happiness, pain and relief, sympathy, pride...

Meeting Mildred in Wales brought her clarity about her mother's life in their home, her fragile state of mind and her attachment to Byron... It was painful to realize that her mother didn't have any other choice but to cling to the one who took ownership of her destiny since the day she arrived. With the best of intentions, or not, he had no right to steer the course of the life of a girl in strained circumstances, facing an inestimable loss.

Nevertheless, until the end of her life her mother still believed he was a good and kind man. Possibly!

Sabrina filled the void in her heart through Mildred's words, and reflecting about her father, now she knows who he really was, a kind and generous man who left many good deeds... But, in her opinion, he was also selfish and manipulative.

Experiencing the surroundings as her mother did as a young woman in Merthyr, Cardiff and London, Sabrina came to realize the extraordinary manner in which 'Dinora' adapted to her new lifestyle, considering her primary roots in a simple, undeveloped place like the one in Greece.

Everything became very clear to Sabrina as she came to a full understanding of her mother's past history, she finally put the pieces of her life together.

Her determination to keep looking for her uncle ended in triumph! A bittersweet but exhilarating feeling. The accomplishment of having found Dimitri was the most significant source of joy and at the same time sadness for her mother never having him back in her life.

If Sabrina had only known of him before her mother's demise...

How could two people, a brother and sister who were deeply connected, drift apart so easily?

That traumatic separation, after losing her family, was the cruelest event in her mother's life.

Sabrina went to her mother's room, held the little wooden box of ashes and said words as if she could hear them:

"Mom, I know wholeheartedly you were there with me at every site, at every step, and I found him, I found your brother, my uncle!

Thank you, Mom, you left me him and a family!

You may rest in heavenly peace, Mommy. I miss you so and I will love you for always and always!"

She called Luciana.

"I'm home!"

"I'm happy you are back, and thank you for texting to tell me about your uncle, I'm glad you found him! Bri, you need to tell me everything about him and your new family."

"I will, Luci, come by tomorrow, I have a lot to tell you."

She spent the next morning with Luciana, relating her experiences and findings.

"I can see it on your face, Bri, a calm affect, the serenity of your accomplishment! You did it! You should be proud of yourself!"

She resumed work and told Wyatt, her boss, that her trip was successful!

"Congratulations, Sabrina, good detective work! I haven't seen a smile on your face for a long time."

On Saturday she called Robyn to share, in a long conversation, what she learned in Wales.

"Now I know all about my Mom's life. Mildred was very open about it. She told me all she knew, and the best is, I confirmed Mom was cared for and loved while living with them.

She gave me a picture of my father, it was bittersweet but I finally know how he looked, how he was. I had hoped that I would have the chance to meet him. I'll never see him or hear his voice, he will never hold me and call me his daughter. He died carrying that void in his soul.

Visiting his grave was final.

I also learned that my two half siblings do not know I exist."

"I am very sorry for that, Bri. Did you find any comfort in being in their house?"

"Yes, I did, comfort and healing. Mildred gave me that! She was very kind, I have immense gratitude and admiration for her."

"Tell me about London, your uncle, his family."

"The most exhilarating thing happened when I found my uncle, Uncle Dim is wonderful, just like Mom was.

His daughter, my cousin Norah, has a striking resemblance to my Mom! The entire family embraced me. I have a new family now!"

"I am so happy for you, darling, your determination paid off. Are you going to visit them?"

"Yes, definitely, Uncle Dimitri is also planning to come here to see me. Anyway, I'll see him in Greece next summer, he wants to come with me to bring Mom's ashes, he feels like it is his duty to bring her home, and he is motivated to see his homeland one last time."

Sabrina held on to the report Dimitri gave her for a few days. She knew it was difficult, but she needed to know the truth about what happened in Pherula that culminated in the termination of the entire family.

That was the last piece of history that her Mom never knew!

Finally, she read the report:

'The Greek Authorities were notified of the attack in Pherula in the spring of 1975. Initially they believed that it was somehow related to political disputes that both governments, Turkish and Greek, were having at that time in consequence of the previous Turkish invasion of Cyprus. However, after knowing more facts they considered the attack on the island of Evia unrelated and proceeded with an investigation.

According to the Authorities' conclusive records, Kostas Pheris started his arms trafficking activities in the early sixties, maintaining constant trips between the Greek Islands, Cyprus, Turkey and Syria, activity that he expanded over the years, in partnership with Khan, a Turkish man, that produced them great fortune.

The Police and Greek Coast Guard were unaware of his illegal practice that went under the radar for a long time, and Kostas felt he was above the law of the land.

In the seventies a rebel militia group threatened to take over his business, eliminating Kostas as the middleman. It was confirmed that the coup was orchestrated by Khan, Kostas' own partner, who had made an attempt in open seas, attacking his well equipped boat with no success a month before the attack in Pherula.

In March 1975, the group invaded the property and executed the entire Pheris family, including the minor children. It was known to the local population that two of Kostas' children were in school in England. Their fate is still unknown.

The Pheris property became the rebels' hideout, as they took over Kostas' illegal operation. They did not destroy the village but threatened the villagers, demanding that they stay quiet and supply them with food.

To preserve their lives the villagers abided by their demands, providing the invaders with supplies. In the meantime, secretly, they were appealing to the Authorities in Chalkis to come and banish the rebels from their land.

At the end of 1976 the Army attacked the Pheris property with grenades, further destroying it, killing some of the intruders, arresting others and confiscating the boat.

After that second attack the house became inhabitable.

The villagers were left to continue with their business as usual, cultivating the grove and fishing. A group of them formed a Community Commission and requested ownership of the grove and the port, claiming that there were no other heirs remaining.

About eight years after the tragic assassination of the Pheris family, and assuming that the two remaining children were also eliminated, the land was officially awarded to the Community Commission of Pherula.

Attached to this report are copies of official documents, including a list of the names and presumed ages of the victims of the 1975 attack.

They were buried in a dry well on the plateau.'

***

Sabrina felt sick to her stomach! She couldn't go on reading the list of names.

It was difficult to accept the fact that Kostas, her grandfather, was ambitious beyond limits, he was not like the others who labored and loved their land above all.

She imagined how much that hurt her uncle realizing that his father was an arms smuggler and in the end responsible for the assassination of his entire family. It was horrifying! Poor innocent people, and the children, they all paid the price for Kostas' misguided ambition.

She called Dimitri.

"I read it and I am so sorry, it hurt me, and I can imagine how it hurt you. I understand now why you never went back to claim the property. Uncle Dim, do you feel conflicted about going back?"

"Thank you, Sabrina. I was conflicted for a long time, avoiding to talk about it with my family. Until you appeared, my sons and daughter didn't know my original name or the village I came from. But I am not conflicted anymore, in that primitive, beautiful place there was life and love.

My mother and my sister left a legacy, the villagers adored them. They loved our home, and I completely agree that my sister should be there. We are closing the circle.

All I want to remember are the happy times we had, and I also want to see my homeland one last time...

Tell me when you are ready to go to Greece. As I told you the best time is from April to October, when the flowers are in bloom!"

"I'll schedule my vacations for next summer and I'll confirm, Uncle Dim."

Sabrina reflected how that senseless tragedy affected their lives enormously. How much that brother and sister hurt! And in the end, alone, they were both able to overcome the tragedy and triumph in their personal lives.

Acknowledging what her mother and her uncle went through she realized how people sometimes get wrapped up in the smallness of things, ignoring what is most important in life: love, unity and family.

She was glad she had told her Mom, countless times, how much she loved and admired her! Even without knowing the extent of the struggle she had endured…

Her Mom was not there anymore to tell the Pheris family story, but Sabrina vowed they would not be forgotten.

Robyn invited Sabrina and Shelton for the holidays, he offered to drive her.

On their way to the Cape he wanted to know more about her findings about Blythe's life in Wales.

Sabrina spoke in more detail.

"Mildred enlightened me!"

"I'm not surprised, Sabrina. Analyzing the evidence, from what your mother wrote, what Mildred said and the letters that Byron wrote, I can only conclude he was a manipulator, disguised as a 'sweet persuader' as Mildred referred to him, he took advantage of the state of mind Blythe was in.

I wish she had confided in me, I would have told her I admired her strength in breaking away, and like you I understand why she loved him. I am sorry she carried guilt and shame for their relationship, when she was not responsible for it."

"Yes, it would have made a difference to us if Mom had the time to write about her first decade here in Boston, how she dealt with those feelings and memories until she met you, Shelton, and started the best relationship of her life, as she used to say. Mom did love you."

"There was a time in the past when I believed the reason she didn't want to marry me was because she never got over the loss of your father. I assumed he had died, and that was the reason she had left Wales.

I wanted the commitment of a marriage with her, the mutual support, sharing common goals, I thought it was what she had before, I was wrong! In reality she was scarred by the illegitimate relationship they had."

"You are right, after learning about Mom's past I came to the same conclusion, when she finally decided to leave him she became her own person and did not want to create dependencies, emotional or otherwise, anymore. But I wish she had married you, Shelton, as a child I dreamed of you being my father…"

"I did want to be your father, Sabrina. And as 'my daughter' I want you to know I miss her, I hurt for her, but I am giving myself a chance, I have visited Robyn a few times, her presence comforts me, we have our love for Blythe in common and we are committed to nurturing our friendship…"

"Are you saying you and Ma Robyn are dating?"

"It is not dating, we are offering the feelings of friendship and affection we had for our mutual friend to each other, it makes us both feel less lonely."

"I understand. It is not fair that you remain alone, and Robyn lost her best friend too, there is nothing wrong in taking care of one another."

"You too, Sabrina, need to move on, keeping your Mom in your heart, but do not be alone… That is not what she wanted for you."

"Shelton, do you think she would want me to be close to my new family?"

"She wanted you to be loved and cared for, I know that for sure."

Christmas at Robyn's was very quiet but pleasant. Two days of sharing memories of their lives with their dear Blythe...

Sabrina could clearly see that her old friends were putting an effort to cheer her up. This was their first Christmas without her Mom, they couldn't forget her for one moment, she was very much present in their hearts and minds.

Back at home Sabrina heard from Luciana. She got an engagement ring, as expected, but she was frustrated because Jonathan was reluctant to set their wedding date.

She gave her fiancé a deadline, she wanted the wedding to be next September, when they complete their fifth anniversary together.

"Bri, I need to make a decision, what do I do? I don't want to lose Jon, but we can't go on like this forever. Honestly I don't understand why he is so reluctant to set our wedding date."

"Luci, I think you need to see the real reason behind his excuses. What is really going on with Jonathan?"

"I know, I am afraid of digging too deep…"

"Whatever happens I am here to support you, Luci."

"Anyway you are not spending New Year's alone, come to my

house."

"I don't feel like celebrating, Luci. I'd rather be alone."

"Not at all, you are joining us. We'll have some wine, listen to music. No loneliness, no tears tonight!"


The Thanov family called from England. Dimitri told her he was planning to visit her soon.

"Sabrina, I know that the one year anniversary is coming up, I want you to know that I am thinking of you and my sister. I want to come and see you by the end of the month, I could stay for a week. Is January a good month to come?"

"It is terribly cold here in the winter, Uncle Dim, but I would love to have you at home. Is Aunt Layla coming too?"

"Cold! It's alright, we will be indoors most of the time, talking, we have much to catch up on. Layla apologizes, she avoids flying long distances, she has panic attacks."


On the anniversary of her mother's death, Sabrina went into her room, looked around.

One year had gone by, it felt like it happened yesterday… And she hasn't taken anything away, yet.

'It is time to let go of things, the life and the love she gave me will last forever.'


Robyn called her.

"I am thinking of her and you today. How are you feeling, Bri?"

"I am strong, Ma Robyn, I made a decision, I am going on with my life, keeping my Mom in my heart but it does not have to hurt anymore."

"That is what she most wanted for you, darling."

"My uncle is coming by the end of the month and I would like you to meet him. Do you want to plan for us to come to the Cape or do you want to come to Boston?"

"I was thinking of coming to Boston anyway. Remember last year I spent a few weeks with you? I would like to do the same this winter again."

"Oh, please come, Ma Robyn, this house is empty and sadder in the winter…"

Dimitri arrived on a frigid and snowy day.

Sabrina was delighted to see him again.

"Can you believe this is the first time in my life that I have family staying over? We had friends, dear friends, I'll be introducing you to them. Robyn, my godmother, Mom's best friend of all, is coming, and I'll invite Shelton to join us. He also wants to meet you."

"Shelton, her boyfriend? Why didn't they marry?"

"Mom didn't want any attachments or dependencies with men. I came to understand why."

"What about you, Sabrina, do you feel the same way? Do you have any significant man here in Boston?"

"No, I don't feel the same way. Before I went to London I let go of a boyfriend that I loved but was not so significant after all. But I hope someday I'll find the right one."

"There are plenty of good men in England who would love to meet someone like you…"

"Are you trying to set me up, Uncle Dim? I am not looking for anyone right now… I need to make decisions about Mom's things. Should I continue living here?"

"Would you consider relocating, coming to live with your family? Think about it, Sabrina, from my side I can't imagine going forward knowing that my only niece is far away, alone, you are part of us!"

"It is nice to hear that, Uncle Dim, I'll think about it. It is tempting, but I would not make a rushed decision."

"In time, my dear, you will make the best decision for yourself, your Mom would want what is best for you, and so do I."


Later, after he rested:

"Uncle Dim, tell me when you are ready to see Mom's room."

"I am ready to visit with my sister now."

Sabrina opened the door. Before he stepped in the room he looked around.

"It has her colors! Feels like she is here."

He walked straight to the window.

The little box of ashes was placed on the round table by the window, where Sabrina had arranged fresh flowers.

"Dinora always loved yellow flowers…" He pointed to the box.

"May I hold it?" His eyes were watery.

"Of course!"

As he held the box close to his heart he broke into tears. He was very emotional.

"Oh my sister, my beloved sister."

Sabrina held his arm and sat with him on the edge of the bed. She embraced him.

"I have done this so many times, Uncle Dim, holding her and crying... You have waited forty years to be reunited with your sister, and it is devastating that it has to be this way. I am so sorry!"

"It was all my fault that I lost her, she trusted me, she was just a girl, I did not make the right decision when I sent her away alone to Wales, then I really didn't do a good job trying to find her. I failed my sister. I regretted it for so long. She suffered, I suffered, it was all in vain."

"Don't blame yourself, Uncle Dim. There is no explanation for what happened, fate was working against both of you. You were both young and inexperienced, how could you have foreseen the consequences?"

He cried for a while.

Then Sabrina showed him the desk.

"Mom spent hours, days, years writing at this desk, all of these drawers are filled with her papers. The shelves downstairs are crowded with her books, some she wrote, they are currently being used in universities!

And here, her closet, with everything, I didn't dispose of anything yet. If there is something that you would like to keep as a remembrance of her, you can take it."

"Thank you, Sabrina, I love this space, I feel her presence here. May I stay in this room?"

"Yes, of course."

Their first day together was bittersweet. He told her stories of his childhood in Pherula.

"Strangely enough most of my memories are from early childhood, maybe because that was the age of wonderment, when all the things around us were magical! And in every single memory Dinora is present!"

The next day Sabrina told him, "Tell me when you feel ready to go outside, there is not much sightseeing we can do in the freezing cold, but there are some very beautiful places in Boston that you might enjoy.

Uncle Dim, for dinner tonight we are invited by my Portuguese friends across the street. Manuela, my best friend's Mom, is a great cook, her father Pedro is a gentleman, they are very welcoming, you'll enjoy meeting them.

We have been friends since Mom and I moved into this house, and this past year they have been exceptionally caring to me."

During his stay Sabrina showed him some of Boston's sites.

"It's your first time in my hometown, and one of the things that you can't miss is the fabulous top view of the city from the Skywalk Observatory, especially at night, it's really beautiful!

You are in the food business, so you might also enjoy going to a few of our best restaurants, and maybe do some wine tastings, Uncle Dim!"

"I agree with all of that, Sabrina, just don't take me ice skating or skiing… I wouldn't survive that." He laughed.

"No! But on Saturday I would love to bring you to Cambridge, it's just across the river from here."

"That's something I would love to see, Harvard."

"Yes, Mom and I crossed that bridge often, we love it there. We can have some hot chocolate in Harvard Square and also visit the Cambridge Antique Market, that was one of Mom's favorite places!"

"That would be lovely. I might find something special to take home to Layla, she loves antiques and arts."

Uncle and niece went out a few times, he was most interested in knowing about her childhood experiences around town. She told him many stories of her and her mother.

"There are memories of Mom all over, wherever I look, wherever I go, I see her… She loved this city and had great joy exploring around."

"It is good to know that Dinora connected to this place and had a good life here."

"She did! She was very successful professionally, she moved into the neighborhood of her choice, she found love, she had a full life. Mom loved the change of seasons, even in the winter she would have a blast after a snowfall, with the excuse of shoveling snow she would take me out of the house to play with her, to make snowballs, snowmen.

Mom had a joy to her, a childlike quality, we had much fun together!

For all twenty-eight years she lived in Boston she smiled quite a lot. I didn't suspect that behind her beautiful smile there were tragic memories..."

"I'm delighted to know Dinora was like our mother, she too had much fun with us and admired all things around. She had a special appreciation for nature, all that we experienced with her made her unforgettable!"

Robyn arrived. She gave Dimitri a big hug.
"So nice to meet my best friend's brother."
Shelton joined them, and for hours they had great conversation.

Dimitri liked them very much, he told his niece:
"They are great people. You are right, Sabrina, they are like family.
I would be so happy if Dinora had married Shelton and he would be your father."
"I'm not really alone, Uncle Dim, Mom brought some wonderful people into my life."

The day before Dimitri was getting ready to leave he had a sensitive discussion with his niece.
"Please don't think I am crazy, Sabrina, I am feeling that I can't leave her behind. You know how I took care of my sister when we were young, I would love to have guardianship of her at least for a little while...
It might be difficult for you but please allow me to bring her ashes. I'll keep her in my home until we meet in Greece in the summer."

"Will that make you feel better, Uncle Dim? It is hard to let her go, sooner or later…"

"Over forty years ago she left Greece with me to go to London, now I want us to return together, for the last time. It closes the circle, I mean, it brings me closure."

Sabrina got emotional.

"She'll be in good hands, you can take her with you, Uncle Dim. That is the reason I found you, wasn't it? For you to be reunited and part of our lives, and you'll help me fulfill her last wish, you know the way home."

Dimitri left, Sabrina was sad, they had bonded.
She missed him.

Robyn stayed with Sabrina for another week.

"I am glad you are here with me, Ma Robyn. I have something difficult to do during this long winter! I need your help to make a decision about Mom's belongings. I can't hold on to everything, it is part of the process of letting go."

"It's just the right time, Bri, you have waited over a year… I can help you with the things in her closet, have you taken what you are going to keep?"

"I did, I took her favorite English black trench coat and this oversized cashmere sweater that she wore every day in the house. It still has her scent.

If you find anything that brings you a good memory of Mom, you may keep it, Ma Robyn. Everything else needs to be packed, Luciana volunteered to take care of what we are going to donate."

"Alright, Bri, you don't need to worry about this, tomorrow while you are at work I'll spend the day bagging and packing."

"Oh, thank you, Ma Robyn. That helps me very much."

The next couple of days Robyn took care of everything. The room looked bare.

Before she left, Sabrina told her:
"It is overwhelming to be in this house alone, it feels empty. For a moment I thought of asking you to leave Scotty, for company, someone waiting for me when I come home, but it quickly became

a bad idea… He is happy with you, Ma Robyn, you give him much more time and attention than I can."

"And I am happy with him, darling. Come and see us soon."


Luciana came over, and Sabrina told her friend about letting her uncle take her mother's ashes to England.

"I feel like I am missing my Mom even more. Now, she is really gone."

"Aren't you losing it a little bit? Letting him travel with her ashes to England?"

"You don't know how much my Mom loved her brother, if she were here she would be so happy to go home with him. She is not here, this is all symbolic! I did it for him too. I know, Luci, it is hard to understand unless you are experiencing it.

Don't look at me like I am losing my mind, I don't want to lose your friendship over this, I already lost a boyfriend…"

Luciana laughed.

"No, you are not losing me, never. I really understand. And the boyfriend… you deserved much better. His loss!"


Sabrina's work was very intense but she was able to schedule two weeks of vacation for the beginning of June.

"Where are you going this time?" Wyatt asked her.

"I am taking my Mom's ashes to Greece, her final resting place."


She confirmed to her Uncle she would meet him in Athens on the second day of June.


She spoke with Luciana:

"I have been thinking, my uncle invited me to come and live with them, I also have to figure out what to do with my house, it is too big for me alone and crowded with memories…

Oh, I have so much to consider and resolve."

"I understand, Bri, if I didn't have my parents and if my aunt in Portugal would ask me to join them, I would move in a heartbeat! In the end family is all that matters, but how am I going to live without you, if you go?"

"If I go, Luci, you'll always have a permanent place in my life, you are like a sister to me!"

"You are going to be here for my wedding, aren't you?"

"Of course I will! I would never miss your wedding."

"In that case let's go shopping, Bri, I am very nervous about finding the right dress. I need your opinion."

Luciana told her about a bridal store in Watertown where she could get a designer dress off the rack. She made an appointment, and the two best friends went on Saturday morning.

Initially they were having fun, but it got to a point that Luciana, seeing herself in the mirror in a beautiful gown, broke into tears.

Surprised by her friend's reaction, Sabrina asked her:

"Why are you crying, Luci? You look so beautiful! Don't you like the dress?"

Luciana ran to the fitting room to take it off. She returned and they left the store.

"Bri, I am afraid my wedding is not going to happen, Jonathan is getting cold feet, he thinks we are rushing into it, maybe next year, he says…"

"Oh my! I didn't see this coming, I thought you were a strong couple. Luci, is there anything I can do or tell you to make you feel better?"

"Maybe you can give me some of your confidence, you don't shy away from making decisions, you are not afraid of the unknown… I am! What if I never love anyone like I love Jon, what if I never marry?"

"Is that what is holding you back? He is not reassuring you. Do you think he feels the same way?

Tell him everything you are feeling, Luci, that's all I can say! Don't be afraid!"

Sabrina invited Shelton over.

"I know Mom discussed many projects with you, and I need your help sorting out the books that you want for yourself and the ones we should donate to the University Library.

I am keeping her legacy, all of her writings and publications."

"It is going to take us days, Sabrina, but this is something I would like to be involved with, all of these books were especially important to Blythe."

He helped her immensely with that task. Days later there were many boxes, some for her to keep and others that Shelton was going to bring to the library.

She looked at the empty shelves.

"That's all there is! In the end there is a void. No one would ever fill it. That part of my life with my Mom is over, now I have an empty space and just memories, sweet, loving memories.

Oh, Shelton, I adored my mother. Sometimes I ask myself, why did she have to leave so soon and suddenly?"

"Life is not fair, Sabrina, that's life! I feel the same way…"

She had spoken to her uncle a few times since he left.

Dimitri told her how grateful he was to her for allowing him to have his sister's ashes for the past few months.

"It was like a return to the past! I was filled with melancholic memories of us, of sadness and also of pure love and gratitude.

When I arrived in Manchester I placed the box on the fireplace mantel for all to see, reunited the family and told them that was a joyous event, my sister finally came home, and we prayed in reverence:

'Beloved sister, may your spirit in Heaven receive our love, now and for always.'

The next time I was in London I brought her along, Layla didn't like the idea, she thought I was out of my mind, but all I wanted was to walk to a few places around the city, reliving memories of what once my sister and I experienced together in our youth."

"I understand, Uncle Dim, we all grieve in different ways, there is no right or wrong."

"Holding the bag with the little box inside, I took a cab here and there and did some walks around London. Went to where we used to live, then to the College, saying, 'Here we are together again, little sister.'

It was cathartic! After forty-one years, now I am ready to bring her home and say goodbye.

Thank you, Sabrina, for this opportunity! Thank you for understanding."

A few days before the trip she called her uncle.

"I am all set, Uncle Dim! We will meet at the Athens Airport, and I have a surprise for you! I'll be returning to London with you!"

"Happy news! I am glad you are flying with me! For how long are you staying with us?"

"For another week or so."

"Layla and the rest of the family will love to see you here."

"We are in this together, Uncle Dim! Meet you in Athens! My first time in Greece and I am happy you are going to be my guide!"

## CHAPTER SIX

# EMOTIONAL JOURNEY

$S$abrina arrived at the Athens Airport and waited for her uncle. His flight landed one hour later and he came, holding his carry-on with the precious box.

Uncle and niece were reunited again!

"Did you pick up your luggage, Sabrina?"

"I did, Uncle Dim, and put it in a locker here at the airport. All I need is this backpack and my hiking boots, just for a few days."

"You are right, smart girl! Let's embark on this adventure. I did this so many times in the past, now one last time. I am ready to go to Pherula!"

"Do you need to rest first, Uncle Dim?"

"I am energized, but I think we should rest on the island before we rent a car to drive east to Steni. I am very anxious to get there."

They went from Athens to the coast and crossed the bridge to Chalkis. They were both jet lagged, it was late in the afternoon, and they decided to spend the night to proceed early the next morning.

He rented a Jeep.

"The road to Steni is pretty good, but once we turn to Pherula it's very rugged. I doubt that any significant improvements have been made in the area."

From the very beginning, Sabrina started experiencing a familiarity with the surroundings, she had heard of them before, in her mother's writings!

During the ride Dimitri told his niece that in the region they spoke a kind of dialect which was difficult to understand even for native Greek speakers.

She had read that before, too.

"I haven't had many opportunities of speaking Greek, but I will be fine, what you learn in childhood will stay with you for always."

"I feel very illiterate around here, Uncle Dim, I can't read those letters or characters... I couldn't do it without you."

They arrived in Steni and stopped to look around for a while before continuing.

He remarked, "Time stood still, it all looks the same here! Now the arduous journey starts!"

And hard it was, but beautiful. Throughout the entire way, fields of dried rocky soil and roadsides covered by wild flowers of all colors growing up into the hillsides made an amazing spectacle of natural views that man hadn't touched.

"Those flowers, bushes and shrubs are resistant to drought and neglect, they bloom year after year," he said.

They finally arrived at the olive grove.

Initially she had the impression that hundreds of old trees were lifeless with dried twisted branches, but in contrast, they were full of green leaves and fruit, and under the immense extension of olive trees by the hillside there were flowers, and more flowers, defying the inclement soil.

"The grove looks the same, nothing has changed! Those bushes with the maturing bean pods are lupines! They are also covered with flowers in the spring."

"I know, lupini beans, my Mom ate them, it was her favorite snack! I thought they were from Italy."

"They grow all over the Mediterranean region and here they grow wildly, and for always. The locals call these flowering plants perennials, I used to call them eternals!"

They reached a narrow parking area with two old trucks.

"This is our final destination, from here across the grove we can walk a couple of kilometers or travel by donkey into the village."

"Donkey! Those donkeys over there?"

A man was approaching and spoke to Dimitri.

"He wants to give us a ride, a donkey ride."

"What do you mean? Do we sit on the donkey, and the man guides it? I think I prefer to walk, I am afraid to fall off the animal."

Dimitri laughed like she never saw before, a big loud laugh, even the man, who certainly did not understand what she said, laughed too.

"Are you afraid of the animal? Oh, city girl, it is a long and treacherous walk."

"Did my Mom sit on the backs of donkeys?"

"Yes, she did, she loved them, she talked to them…"

"It's OK, Uncle Dimitri, I'll walk."

Dimitri took one donkey, he attached his luggage to another, and they started walking slowly.

"If this place is so primitive, where are we going to stay overnight, are we going back to Steni?"

"Don't worry, every village has a house where they rent a room for transients."

"Who is going to transit around here?"

"Business people, the ones who negotiate the crops, goat products or fish."

She was very impressed with the mix of beauty and wild roughness.

There was a crystal clear natural spring running down the

mountains into a creek.

Dimitri told her, "Look what they did, they piped it! How smart! We used to come here with buckets to bring water home, and sometimes we had a lot of fun bathing in the falls."

"Bathing? Must be so cold!"

"Refreshing, especially on a warm summer day."

"How are you feeling, Uncle Dimitri, are you well?"

"I am emotional, it is all real, I am really here! I am anxious with the anticipation of meeting old friends from my past, people that I grew up with, people that I loved! My heart is racing, Sabrina."

"Mine is too, it's like being in a dream, Uncle Dim!"

She was tired of the difficult walk through the hills, but did not complain.

When they had the first view of the village, she exclaimed:

"Look at that! It's astonishing! All of those rows of houses built together out of stones, rocks, and the walkway is paved, it's beautiful, and much bigger than I had imagined!"

"It's not paved, Sabrina, it is naturally rocky."

As they approached, villagers started coming out, men, women, children greeting the visitors, saying unintelligible words, waving their hands.

"They are so welcoming!"

They arrived at the final stop, Dimitri came down from the donkey and gave the man a few coins.

Another man approached. Dimitri asked him where the 'Inn' was. He held his carry-on and they followed him.

As they walked through the alleyway, all of a sudden they started feeling the breeze and seeing a partial view of the sea.

"Look, Uncle Dimitri! The sea!"

"We will have a full view from the plateau. We'll get there!"

They stopped at one of the houses, a woman came out, she was about Dimitri's age. She guided them in and offered a very modest room with two simple beds. She showed them the bathroom outside and brought them to a dining area furnished only with a rustic table and benches, and offered them fruit, cheese and bread.

"I want to refresh a little and drink some water, you should rest too, Uncle Dimitri, before we walk some more."

"I will, Sabrina. What do you think so far?"

"Amazing experience, unlike any other. Imagining is one thing but seeing is another. I can relate to my mother's description, and seeing it with my own eyes I have the feeling I have been here before."

A man came into the house and stared at Dimitri, he approached Ileana, their hostess, and said a few words.

Dimitri told his niece:

"He is asking his wife if she knows me, he thinks I look familiar, so does he, I remember him, Orion was a grove worker."

The man kept looking at them. At a certain point he shouted out loud, "Dimitri! Dimitri Pheris!" He said something else and came hugging him, in tears. Dimitri exchanged a few words with him and then introduced him to Sabrina, "Dinora's daughter!"

The man hugged her and kissed her face. She was paralyzed.

"Don't be afraid, Sabrina, they loved your mother, Orion was one of our friends, they are very happy to see us."

Ileana also hugged and kissed them, repeatedly. Then she went outside the house shouting, and other people started coming and greeting them with affection.

Dimitri talked to the people and answered their questions. Then he told them what he was there for... Some cried.

Word spread fast in the little village about Dimitri's appearance. He excused himself, telling the people he wanted to show the remains of the *frurio* and the sea cliff view to his niece.

The villagers gave them privacy, solemnly lining up the path between the houses while Sabrina and Dimitri walked through.

"Why are they all crying, Uncle Dimitri?"

"They are emotional, they never expected me back. Orion asked me if I came to claim the land, I said no, it belongs to them. Then I told him I came only to bring my sister's ashes, he cried too.

Dinora taught some of these people how to read and write. They never forgot her."

"When do you want to do this, Uncle Dimitri? It is getting late, isn't it?"

"We will do it tomorrow morning, but I want to show you the *frurio* and the cliff now."

As they walked along the stone-paved alley a bright view of the sea opened up in front of their eyes, down at the right side there was the port with a small fishing boat anchored.

Going down below to the port there was the rocky cliff wall, covered with bushes of yellow flowers. On the left side, a few steps up to the plateau, they saw the remains of the *frurio*. After the destruction no one had rebuilt it.

Dimitri couldn't contain his tears, neither could Sabrina, and she could only whisper, "Breathtaking! Amazing view!"

'I am seeing it with my very own eyes! Just like you said, Mommy! A picture I had in my mind,' she sighed.

"I never forgot this view!" he told her.

Together, they walked down the carved steps. The tide was low, there was a little piece of rough sand exposed, she sat on the rock, took her hiking boots and socks off, and stepped down into the water.

Dimitri observing, told her, "I see Dinora playing in the water again…"

She looked around at the profusion of polished rocks and pebbles, she got a black shiny one and brought it to him.

"For your collection, Uncle Dimitri." He smiled between his tears.

She wet her hands and brought them to her face. "The Aegean Sea's pure water."

In every second of this experience they felt like Dinora was there with them!

She put her boots on, and they went up to the plateau for a full view of what was left of the *frurio*. Some partial columns were still standing, they walked around.

The view from there to the open sea was more than the word magnificent could say. Mesmerizing!

Dimitri touched a column, leaned his head against it and cried profusely. Sabrina put her arm around him, she understood his pain. That was the place he was born, his home, and now a mount of ruins. It was a moment of deep respect for the place and for all the lives lost there.

He composed himself, then described it: "There were not many rooms, this was the larger one where we all gathered, ate, slept."

"Why do you think the villagers did not rebuild it?"

"Because this is now sacred ground, they are all buried here."

In every direction they looked, there were bushes of blooming flowers coming out of the soil between the rocks.

Her uncle showed her the dry well in the courtyard covered with engraved stones. He touched each one of them.

"What does that mean, Uncle Dimitri?"

"This is our family tomb. Probably after the invaders were gone the villagers engraved the stones with the names of the ones buried here. These large characters mean Pheris, the Pheris family, this one is Pappous, this is Adina, my mother, my sweet, loving mother, this one is Kostas, my father, this is Spiros, my older brother, and his wife Nyla, and their children Atlas, Lassis, Thasos and Calliah, and this is Kaia! Kaia?"

"Who was Kaia, Uncle Dimitri?"

"She was my girlfriend, my first love, Orion's sister! I'm surprised he didn't mention anything about her... I'll ask him."

He touched with loving care each rock, every letter, every character, while tears were rolling down his face.

Sabrina supported her uncle and shared his deep emotion.

"I am so sorry for all of them, for you, for Mom. I am so sorry! I understand now why this is sacred ground, I feel a sense of reverence honoring their lives. Mom would say *'riverenza,'* she used to express major emotions or events in old, classic words.

*'Riverenza'* is the proper expression to describe this profound feeling of respect for their lives and this place!"

In contrast with their stone surroundings there were beautiful bushes covered with delicate flowers coming out of the ground all around the well, now the gravesite.

"This was simply a hole in the ground, Pappous built a wall

around it so we didn't fall into it while we played as children, it was our little piece of Heaven," he said.

"Mom called it 'Mother Earth's womb.' I feel compelled to take a small piece of this place that will last forever, a tangible memory. Do you mind, Uncle Dim?"

"Not at all, I think it is a good idea, I'll take one too."

Both uncle and niece looked around for the perfect piece of rock to take along. The rocks of all sizes had a yellowish tone. Sabrina took one that didn't have sharp edges, about the size of half a brick, and Dimitri took a little larger one.

"I used to collect rocks and stones when I was a boy… This one will have a place of honor in my home."

The villagers stayed in silence at a distance, they did not come to the plateau, as a sign of respect.

Dimitri and his niece walked towards them, leaving the restricted area. "We will be back tomorrow morning."

They walked in silence while people followed them. A little girl approached and led the way, holding Sabrina's hand, and all of a sudden some other children surrounded her and started shouting…

"What are they saying, Uncle Dim?"

"They want to hear your voice, talk to them."

As they approached the house a lot of people were around, smiling, shaking their hands. One of the men talked to him:

"Dimitri, remember me? I am Corban! Your sister taught me to read and write, and when you went to school in Chalkis she started teaching us English too. Some of the children can understand, at least a little. Ask Dinora's daughter to talk to them."

Dimitri embraced him, "Corban, I remember you and your father, he was the one who called me in London with the devastating news after the invasion."

"Yes he did, he felt it was his obligation to protect you and your sister from that calamity."

Dimitri asked Sabrina, "Do you know a verse or something to tell the children? They want to hear you, some of them understand a little English."

"This is where my law school skills don't serve me for

anything! I do not know poems, but there is a song that I learned in kindergarten that stayed with me over the years and right now well represents what I am feeling about this place and these people."

Corban translated to the crowd, and the children started shouting: "Sing! Sing! Sing!"

"Tell the youngsters the song comes with gestures, sign language, and they can follow me, and I'm sorry for my poor singing... The man who made this song immortal was an adored artist, in my head I still can hear him singing:

*'I see trees of green, red roses too,*
*I see them bloom for me and you,*
*And I think to myself, what a wonderful world...'*

The children mimicked her gestures, accompanying the song lyrics, and at the end, they asked for more and more... She sang it repeatedly.

That was an unforgettable experience of joy shared with the children, who were all smiles and continued repeating the gestures long after they had left.

Dimitri told her, "I have you on record, I am going to show it to the whole family, you were so sweet, you gave them the same demonstration of love for this place as your mother used to. And you can sing!"

"It came from my heart, for them and for my Mom, it was one of her favorites..."

There were lights on inside the Inn.

"I didn't see any power lines!"

"Time of progress, I observed that there are generators everywhere. In my time only the *frurio* had a generator by kerosene, now looks like there are many around."

Ileana, their hostess, had prepared a table full of fruit, breads and sauces, cheeses and olives, all sorts of olives. There was also roasted lamb, which Sabrina rejected.

"I hope I am not offending them, Uncle Dim, sorry I can't eat the little animal..."

A few men, older and younger than Dimitri, among them Orion

and Corban, waited to talk to him.

They told him how the village prospered with their management and that they were able to share with him how they obtained ownership.

"It is a cooperative, it belongs to all of us, we all work on it."

Dimitri expressed his satisfaction with how they cultivated the land, and he reassured them that the grove was rightfully theirs.

"I always knew that many of you are also Pheris relatives. It is in the right, good hands!"

He asked Orion, "I saw Kaia's name by the grave among the others. What happened to her?"

"She was at the *frurio* with your mother the day the attack happened, she became another innocent victim."

"I am very sorry, Orion, you know she was my first love..."

"I know. We will talk more about her later."

Orion was emotional.


Corban told Dimitri that in the last decades many of the youngsters had left for other opportunities in larger villages and towns.

"From all the children that you see here now, three out of four will leave. But we accept others moving in, as we need more people working.

This village will never die, it has been here for centuries and will remain for many more."

"I am glad to know that, Corban! And I am glad this land belongs to all of you, you'll cultivate the grove and will tell the next generations the stories of how it all started."

Orion interrupted:

"Yes! We have journals filled with stories, we found them in the *frurio* among other objects, after the invasion. Did you write them, Dimitri? Do you want to see them?"

Dimitri felt a chill down his spine.

"Is it possible that those are the stories that Pappous asked Dinora to write?"

"Uncle Dim, Mom wrote the stories, she mentioned that in her script! I'd like to see them!"

Orion brought three old, scuffed up journals, a little burned on the edges. Dimitri started going carefully page by page.

He became emotional again.

"Yes, Dinora wrote all of them! Look, Sabrina, your Mom's handwritten journals in Greek! They are over fifty years old and contain stories of our family for more than two centuries."

As he continued looking carefully through the pages, he said that Dinora had also made some personal entries, telling their own stories.

Sabrina held one of the journals.

"I am so sorry I can't read Greek. Oh, my Mom wrote them! They are precious and priceless!"

Dimitri spoke to Orion and Corban.

"This is the Pheris family history, the founders of this land, my family! My sister wrote them as Pappous told us. This is my only heritage from our family. I want to buy them. Please, name your price."

The men discussed it for a little while. Orion and Corban were compliant. Sabrina was anxious waiting for Dimitri to tell her what they agreed.

He told her:

"They don't want any money from us, they are saying that the community took ownership of the grove, and we should have at least this piece of heritage from our family, they will give us the journals, all they want are copies to continue telling the children how Pherula was founded and built.

Orion will come with us tomorrow to Steni, he wants to talk to me about Kaia, and he will make copies. He said there is a copy machine at the Post Office."

Sabrina got up and hugged both Orion and Corban.

"Thank you, you are wonderful, unselfish men. Oh, my Mom would be so happy for this gift. Thank you!"

Orion had tears in his eyes and told her:

"I kept her books, hoping that she would return someday... I feel great joy to speak to you, Dinora's daughter, you brought her back to us.

When I was a boy Dinora taught us to read and write, and she also taught us English. I continued her mission teaching the youngsters what I had learned. Later as a grown man I went to Chalkis once a week for classes. I did it all for her, I loved her."

Sabrina held his hand.

"Thank you, Orion, love lasts forever!"

Corban told them that the villagers wanted to be part of the funeral ceremony in the morning and they were carving a stone with Dinora's name to be placed with the others.

Dimitri responded, "My niece and I will be honored."

Ileana spoke to Sabrina, her husband translated.

"Ileana was one of your mother's friends, she loved her and always prayed for her. But there is someone next door who has told her that Dinora was coming back, she wants to see you, I mean, she is blind, she is about one hundred years old. She is Manteia, our oracle."

"An oracle? Yes, I'd like to meet her."

Dimitri commented:

"I remember Manteia, she would come to the *frurio* to talk to my mother. I can't believe she is still alive! I want to see her, too."

Ileana accompanied Sabrina and Dimitri two houses down. The oracle was sitting on a bed with her legs covered with a white cotton blanket, everything was white in the room. Ileana spoke to her, Manteia stretched her hands, Ileana held Sabrina's hand and joined them.

Initially she didn't say a word, she held Sabrina's both hands for a while, then stretched her right hand to touch her face and started speaking.

Dimitri translated:

"I've waited for you, beloved child! You spread the seed of knowledge among us, you left us love, and love is immortal."

"Uncle Dimitri, she thinks I am my Mom!"

Manteia put her hand over Sabrina's heart, and continued:

"Her soul lives in you. And you, child of the beloved, will live a long, beautiful life filled with family and love, beyond what you can imagine. Believe it! You will never walk alone.

Let the pain go, for your mother is shining in light! Her spirit is free, watching over you, she guided your steps to the picture on the wall. She rejoices that you brought her home! Blessings to you, beloved child!"

Manteia stretched her hand out to Dimitri, calling him, "Descendent."
She spoke to him for a while.

After they left Dimitri was puzzled and related to Sabrina what the oracle said.
"I believe Manteia is too old to be doing this… not everything she said is true:
'You will become a very old man surrounded by your family, many children to whom you will teach your history. You have denied them the truth about your ancestors.
Your family here on earth is not complete, in finding your long lost son you'll regain pride in your Greek heritage.
Your mother protected you and your sister from the tragedy and she is in peace and in glory.
Redeem yourself, forgive your father!'
She is right, my children know I am Greek, of course, but I never gave them my whole family history, they will know everything that happened here. But a long lost son? Makes no sense."
"Maybe she was just confused, Uncle Dim, but I am astonished she knew about the 'picture on the wall,' that gave me goose bumps!"

They came back to Ileana's house to rest.
"I am glad we are sharing this room, I like to have you around, Uncle Dim. I'm touched by so many emotions today. What a mystical day!"
"So am I, Sabrina. I am reconnecting to this land, to these people, to my own young self, I understand quite well the longing that my sister had to return… We have a mission to complete tomorrow, rest well."
Sabrina held the wooden box, "Our last night together, Mommy."

In the morning while Ileana was serving them a meal, two men came into the house holding a large stone of about twenty pounds, polished and engraved with 'Dinora.'
"We worked all night, this is our homage to your family."

Dimitri and Sabrina thanked them. They stepped outside the house to walk to the burial site.

She held the wooden box tightly against her chest.

The villagers were solemn, lining up along the path, they had flowers in their hands, some women were chanting.

Two young women walking behind them were carrying baskets where the villagers deposited their flowers.

As they approached the plateau to go up a few steps they all stopped. The two men came back from the courtyard.

"We left the stone at the well."

In silence, the villagers respected the privacy of uncle and niece.

Dimitri asked Sabrina, "Let me carry her for this last time."

She gave him the box.

Together they walked into the courtyard and stood by the well.

"Beloved sister, you are home, reunited with our family, where we had an enchanted childhood, playing here with our mother, feeling this breeze and the sunlight on our faces… In our little piece of Heaven!"

He looked at Sabrina, crying.

She placed a kiss on the little box.

"Rest in peace in your 'Mother Earth's womb.' You'll always be in my heart, Mommy! Forever!"

Among the top rocks there was an opening, probably done by the men earlier, where the box fit inside. Dimitri looked at his niece and they didn't have to say a word, they both agreed that was the place.

He put the box deep down, and both of them together lifted Dinora's engraved rock from the ground and placed it perfectly.

They held hands, prayed and said goodbye.

They dried their tears.

Dimitri spoke first.

"The villagers are all waiting for us in silence, as a sign of respect, this is a beautiful demonstration of love."

The young women came and placed the baskets filled with

flowers on the ground, and left. Both niece and uncle spread the flowers all over the tomb and on the ground around it, joining the ones in the blooming bushes.

"I never saw anything this beautiful, all for you, Mommy, and for our family with love and profound respect."

"Dinora Pheris, my beloved sister was born here, she lived her adult life as Blythe Lisvane and now she completes a full circle, returning home as Dinora, as she longed for! Her spirit is soaring to the highest."

They stayed in silence a little longer.
Dimitri took pictures. "Our family in England needs to see this."
Then, holding hands, they walked away.

At the top of the steps he turned to the villagers and said a few words of gratitude.
"I want to say something too, Uncle Dimitri, please translate:
Dear friends, my beloved mother asked me to bring her home.
My Mom lived in and knew many cities of power, of beauty, of magnificent buildings, of universities and castles, but there was no place on this earth that she loved as much as she loved this village.
She loved the sun that is bathing us, the sea that is crashing on the cliff, and the flowers, all the flowers, but most of all she loved you, the people!
I thank you with all my heart for welcoming my mother with much love and respect.
I leave knowing that she rests in peace in this little piece of Heaven, for eternity!"

As they started walking back to Ileana's house a procession of people walked with them until they entered the house. Many waited to follow them outside the village, into the olive grove.
Ileana did not accept any money from Dimitri.
"It was an honor to have you in my house."
Sabrina hugged her and put her own leather jacket on Ileana's shoulders.

"It's yours!"

Ileana broke into laughter and tears thanking her for the present. She had admired and complimented her jacket a few times.

Orion and Corban walked with them to the donkey stop, as did many of the villagers.

A little boy stood by Sabrina and in his broken English started singing: *"I see trees of green, red roses too..."*

She joined him, even Dimitri and some of the older people, and of course the children, sung along.

"Dinora's daughter, you made history here, they will sing it thinking always of you!"

"I am glad I will have this memory, Uncle Dim, I'll remember them and Pherula forever. I feel emotional leaving, knowing that I'll never return."

"Well, you have the memories, and never say never... I also thought I would never return, and here I am, and I am so happy I came. I feel like I finally made amends with my homeland and my family. I always felt guilty that I was not here with them."

After the long way to the Jeep, they left. Orion followed them in his truck.

When they arrived in Steni, Orion asked Dimitri to talk in private. Dimitri told his niece to go to the Post Office across the street and start making copies of the journals.

Orion was nervous, rubbing his hands, and spoke:

"Dimitri, I didn't tell you yesterday in respect of the burial ceremony for Dinora! But now I need to tell you what happened to Kaia.

A couple of months after your last visit in the summer of 1974 she told me she was pregnant, she didn't want to tell our father, and she was waiting for you to come back at the end of the year, she was sure you were going to marry her.

But you didn't come, and I decided to bring her here to Steni, where we had friends and she stayed until her baby boy was born."

"A baby boy, Kaia had a child? My son? I absolutely had no idea, I would have supported her, Orion."

"I know, she knew it too. She returned to Pherula two weeks

later, left the baby with me and my wife, and went to talk to your mother. She was going to tell Adina about the baby, and ask her when you were coming home. That was the day of the invasion."

"Orion, I am shocked, please forgive me for not coming back sooner. Did you raise him? Where is he?"

"I raised him as my own. He was a very smart little boy, but as he grew up he didn't want anything to do with the grove, he loved the sea. I sent him to school in Chalkis, the same school you and Dinora went to.

At the age of seventeen he enlisted in the Navy. He used to say, 'I am a man of the sea.' Today he is a high ranking officer in the Aegean Sea Naval Command in Piraeus. Kaia named him Nikos Dimitri Pheris, she was proud of naming him after you. He is forty-two years old and has two sons."

"He is a Pheris! Does he know about me?"

"He calls me father but he carries the Pheris name with pride. I told him who you were, that you loved my sister, you were committed to her, but we all suspected that you were also killed."

"Orion, I don't know what to say... If the course of my life hadn't changed I would have returned as planned, and with Kaia we would have raised our son together."

"I know, Dimitri, you are a man of honor. We never blamed you, Kaia loved you."

"Does Nikos come to see you often?"

"Not often, but I am sure he would like to meet you."

Orion gave him the address in Piraeus to contact Nikos.

Sabrina came back. She gave Orion two copies of the journals.

"With our eternal gratitude, no money could ever pay for this gift."

Dimitri and Sabrina hugged him, and said goodbye.

Orion went back to Pherula saying:

"Your visit meant much to all of us! Come back someday!"

Before leaving for Chalkis, Dimitri told his niece:

"I can just handle one emotion at a time. Saying goodbye to Pherula was heart wrenching, but what Orion just told me startled me!"

"You look distressed, Uncle Dim. What did he tell you?"

Dimitri related to her his conversation with Orion. Sabrina was equally shocked.

"The long lost son... Manteia was right after all! Are you going to contact him?"

"Yes, I am, I will call the Naval Command once we arrive in Chalkis."

For the rest of the ride Dimitri didn't say a word. Sabrina respected his silence, he was coming to terms with the stunning news he just learned.

Arriving in Chalkis, Dimitri called the Naval Command in Piraeus and was informed that 'Captain Pheris' was away on a mission and would be back in three weeks.

"I'll write to him from London. Before proceeding to Athens I would like to spend some time here, Sabrina, relaxing a little bit."

"Of course, Uncle Dim, and I'd like to go somewhere to charge my phone."

Dimitri chose a café with outdoor tables in a breezy and tranquil place close to the beach.

The sun was shining on the sea.

"Sabrina, sorry I was silent all the way here, I was having a conversation with myself about what we've experienced. I feel calmer now, but in all honesty I feel terribly guilt for the fact that I didn't return earlier when I could and should have.

I moved on, put my entire earlier life in the past, driven by fear and anger, much anger towards my father. Those were the feelings that made me choose not to return, and that was absolutely wrong! Deep inside, like my sister, I always wanted to come back home.

I feel that I was a coward renouncing my heritage, in my mind the entire family was gone! And now, I learned that out of the tragedy, out of the destruction came a new Pheris, a son, and the family lives on.

In a beautiful way, Kaia, a sweet, simple eighteen year old girl, gave birth to the next Pheris generation. My heart is full of love and gratitude for her, and I have to come to terms with my feelings of guilt and shame for having denied my own heritage."

"Uncle Dimitri, we were touched by many emotions these past few days, I understand everything you are feeling and saying, but do not blame yourself, you did what most young people suffering terrible trauma would do. There is no reason to keep nurturing feelings of self-condemnation, there is nothing you can do about the past, look forward, move on, this is a new beginning for you, for your family.

In my heart I am grateful for my Mom, because of her we reunited, and together on this emotional journey we fulfilled her destiny, we found closure, and as a gift you learned that the Pheris family lives on... And maybe that was the reason you came.

I am a firm believer that everything happens for a reason."

"Oh, Little One. You are inspiring, there is a time for tears, and there is a time for healing, from now on I'll honor my past, with much gratitude for everything that life has given me.

But we need to rest now to complete our journey, we are both emotionally exhausted."

They left for Athens in the evening.

The following morning they started an early tour through Athens.

"Are you up for a long walk, Sabrina?"

"So far we have seen some of the places that brought remembrances of you and Mom. I know Athens offers much, I leave it up to you, Uncle Dim, to guide me to wherever you think are the most significant sites."

"I never thought that someday I would be coming back to Greece, showing my niece the places that my sister and I appreciated and enjoyed... I feel an enormous satisfaction doing this.

Athens acquired a universal significance in the past as the historical capital of Europe. As you know there is a multitude of splendid monuments to be seen.

A part of the city's historic centre has been converted into a three kilometer pedestrian route that takes us to the must-see archaeological sites.

My mother, Dinora and I loved to do that, we came many times and had the chance to visit each one of the sites."

"Of course I am up for it, I would love to. Later we can take a cab back to the hotel and get ready for our evening trip. It's perfect, Uncle Dim."

They started around the Acropolis, Temple of Olympian Zeus, Hadrian's Arch, continuing to the ancient Theatre of Dionysus. At every site Dimitri had something interesting to tell.

"You know so much, Uncle Dim. I feel really privileged to learn from you."

"At this moment I'm feeling proud of my Greek heritage. How could I have denied it for so long? I love this land and its history. I have much to share with my children, from now on I won't lament the losses of my loved ones any longer, I will only revere their memories and their legacy."

And they walked and walked, when they sat for lunch Sabrina just had one comment to make:

"Athens is stunning, I am captivated, I would return here to explore more. I also have Greek blood in me, and this experience makes me feel connected to the Greek girl Mom was, and to you..."

Walking right along, they came to the end of the day.

"I have to tell you, Sabrina, that walking with you all day, I felt that I went back in time, decades ago, walking along with my sister, admiring and appreciating these same sites... I feel so much gratitude for all that we shared!"

At the Airport, ready to board, Sabrina told her uncle:

"I can't believe that in only a few days we saw so many unique and beautiful places, met wonderful people, and above all we completed the most meaningful task of our lives, we brought Mom home!"

"We brought her home and in return I had the most unexpected revelation, a son!"

"That's amazing! And I have a very special bond with you, Uncle Dim. This has been for sure a spiritual journey, and I couldn't have done it without you!"

## CHAPTER SEVEN

# *RETURNING HOME*

*O*n the flight to London...

"I am still dumbfounded, I could never imagine learning about a son, a Pheris descendant! I have great respect for Orion, he is a hero, he lived through so much and had it in his heart to raise his children and Nikos, teaching them all to love and respect their land.

I need to write him a heartfelt letter, I didn't thank him enough, and I didn't ask all the questions. I want to know everything about Nikos."

"Would you have married Kaia, if in other circumstances?"

"I would, I was a twenty year old young man in love, I did intend to marry her upon my return from school. I planned to stay in Pherula, working with my father as he wanted."

"Are you going to tell Aunt Layla about Nikos, on your arrival?"

"Definitely, but I need to choose the right time, she will be shocked, maybe as much as I am. In all truth, when I met Layla I did tell her about my first love, Kaia was a lovely girl, she became a sweet memory…"

"For what I know of Aunt Layla, she is profoundly understanding. For her, family matters the most!"

"Indeed, talking about our family can you imagine how happy my sister would be knowing that you are reuniting with us? If you come to live in England it would be like my youngest child is returning home, you would give me much joy."

"Uncle Dim, I need to tell you how significant this experience has been, you are part of my life and there is nothing more that I want than to be close to you and family, but I can't act on an impulse.

In all honesty, I can't make a decision to move to London now, there is much to be considered!"

"I do understand and I have learned, the hard way, what a rushed decision can do to one's life!"

"I am happy to be part of your family and I want to enjoy it. We will always be close, I am not saying no, just not now, I am not ready for that."

"Sabrina, would it be hard to leave Boston? I would make your move as soft as possible, I would help any way I can."

"I have mixed feelings and emotions, Boston is my birthplace, where I grew up, where I went to school, most of all it's the place that I shared with my Mom. My city is filled with memories of her.

I believe I can live in Boston and still maintain a close relationship with our family."

When they were about to land, he asked her:

"Are you staying in London? Maurice offered you to stay with him and Daphne."

"I'd like that, they have such a cute baby!"

"When are you going back home? Did you decide what to do with your house?"

"I'll return in one week, and about my house that was the only decision I made, I will move out eventually, but I am not in a hurry, there is much to be sorted out first, and also my best friend's wedding is in September and that is where I am putting all of my energy for the next months."

"When you move we would help with anything you need to

relocate, that includes money."
"Thank you, Uncle Dimitri, I am alright. All I need is your emotional support."

Arriving in London they went to Maurice's apartment.
Dimitri called Layla.
"I'll be home tomorrow and our Sabrina will come with Norah later this week to see you."
He told his niece, "I will have time alone with Layla to tell her about Nikos, only after that I will tell the entire family. Please don't comment with anyone for now."

Considering that someday she might relocate, Sabrina took an afternoon off to visit her associated office in Central London. She met with management and made professional contacts with the team that she works with remotely, on occasion. They were cordial and welcomed her.

Maurice invited her to his restaurant.
"After that sentimental trip to Greece you need a change of environment. There will be a company party organized by one of my special customers, and you are my guest!"
Sabrina went along with her cousin.

At the dinner party she soon realized that her cousin was not socializing only with customers, he was among friends and he proudly introduced her to many people:
"This is my beautiful American cousin Sabrina."
She talked to some of them until one of the guests showed personal interest in knowing more about her: Edward Brynmair, an architect.
"I almost didn't come to my office party, it is always the same, but I am glad I came to meet an American girl!"
"Sorry to disappoint you but I'm not all American, I am half Greek, half Welsh, born in the USA!"
"Really? Very few people know I am Welsh too! From Aberystwyth. Where is your family from?"
"My father was from Merthyr Tydfil, but I never lived there. I grew up in Boston, Massachusetts, with my Mom, that's where

I've lived until now."

Edward asked her if she had visited her father in Wales.

"I never met my father, but I heard much about him. I visited his tomb only once."

"I am sorry, I shouldn't have asked you."

"It's quite alright!"

They kept the conversation going for a while, he mentioned he had come to London to the Engineering and Architecture College and loved the city so much that he decided to stay.

Edward was charming, his appearance and mannerisms, kind and self controlled tone of voice, reminded her of what she knew about her father's demeanor.

She asked him:

"Are all Welsh men like you? Charming and gentle?"

"Not at all, but I am flattered by your comment."

Before the party was over, Edward asked her:

"What are you doing tomorrow night? I would like to invite you out!"

"I would say yes, I'm enjoying talking to you, Edward."

In the corner of his eye Maurice was observing them talking and smiling, he gave his cousin a thumbs up.

After Edward left she told Maurice:

"I am going to see Edward, he asked me out. How long do you know him?"

"Since we inaugurated the restaurant, his office is close by, he comes here often, I like him, he is a good man, and I had the feeling he would like to meet someone like you."

"You set me up, Maurice! All I can say is I've enjoyed talking to him."

The following evening Edward took her to a quiet and refined dinner at the Ritz. Obviously he wanted to impress her. They talked for hours. He asked many questions about her family and her work, demonstrating great interest in getting to know her.

She told him, "I am a lawyer, international business, and I've worked for the same firm since I was in law school.

Regarding family, I have no one left in the United States, but I have my newfound family here in England. My uncle is insisting that I join them, but I have my career in Boston. Anyway I am thinking about it..."

"If you move to London I would see you all the time. I feel like we have a good connection. What do you say, Sabrina? Do you feel the same way?"

"Edward, we have to consider that long distance relationships are difficult to maintain, but I would also like to keep talking and seeing you."

"I will be in contact with you on every occasion possible and I'll come to see you, if you let me." He kissed her.

They exchanged their information, phone numbers, addresses, emails.

When he dropped her off at Maurice's, they kissed again. She felt very sorry that could be their first and last kisses...

She didn't want that encounter to end, it had been over a year since she had any romantic interest in anyone, until now...

They said goodbye.

On Saturday morning, she went to Manchester with Norah to spend time with her aunt and uncle.

On the way there, Norah told her, "I'll come to visit you in the U.S. one of these days! I mean it! I also want to share with you that I have a new boyfriend. After a long time I found someone worthy and things are really good between us!"

"I wish you the best, Norah! Maybe you'll come with him to the U.S., I'll be glad to be your host."

She spent the most pleasant weekend with her uncle and aunt, reminiscing about their trip to Greece. Aunt Layla told her Dimitri returned a changed man, hopeful and filled with sweet memories about his land and his family.

Before Sabrina left, Dimitri and Layla insisted:

"We hope you can come at the end of December! Please come, Sabrina, we will have the best holiday celebration!"

"Yes, I'll come. First thing I'll do when I resume work is I'll request time off for the holidays. I'll be looking forward to see you all again. I miss you already!"

She called Luciana as soon as she arrived in Boston.

Her friend immediately came to see her.

"I have so much to tell you about my emotional trip to Greece, but from now on I am here for you, Luci. I won't be doing anything else until your wedding!"

Luciana broke into tears.

"I am not sure there'll be a wedding! Jonathan finally told me that he does not care for big ceremonies, a church, guests... He suggested that we elope, only the two of us, he even mentioned that there is a chapel in the state of Maryland where we could just show up and have a legally binding wedding, or maybe go to Las Vegas."

"I can't understand, Luci, you are together for five years and this is the first time he talked about how he feels about the wedding?"

"The very first time! He never told me anything like this before, I tried to convince him that the wedding ceremony, wedding dress, party, it is all very important to my parents, I am their only daughter and I don't want to disappoint them.

I also know that it is very important to his mother as well, she was so excited! I am afraid to say it out loud, but what I really think is that he does not want to marry me and keeps making excuses..."

Luciana was sobbing. Sabrina hugged her.

"I am sorry, Luci, I am so sorry. Are you sure it isn't only anxiety, pre-wedding jitters?"

"I don't know, sometimes I think that's all that it is, then I came to realize that if he really loved me he wouldn't be crushing my dreams and my family's expectations this way."

"Are you considering eloping, Luci?"

"I can't bring myself to do it just because it is convenient for him. If that is how our life as a married couple is going to be, I have much to think about. He made it sound conditional, it is his way or no way! He is being manipulative, don't you think so?"

"I agree, you need to think it over before giving him a final answer, one way or another, in the meantime let's hope that he comes to his senses and everything will be alright."

"It will never be the same, after five years I never thought Jonathan would reveal his feelings about our wedding this way, somehow it chipped away most of my trust in him. I'm afraid this situation is irreparable."

"What can I do, Luci? How can I help you feel better?"

"Maybe we can go out somewhere for the weekend, I know you just came back from your trip and want to be home. I am avoiding him and I need a distraction, and you can tell me all about Greece."

"Of course, I'll call Ma Robyn, she always welcomes us. That's what we are going to do! And I'll have so much to tell her about my experience in the village in Greece, it was mystical! I never experienced anything like that."

The weekend with Robyn was good for all of them. Sabrina told her about her amazement getting to the remote village.

"The most primitive and undeveloped place I had ever seen, filled with pure natural beauty. And the people, I loved them! It was a spiritual experience!

I miss my Mom terribly, but now I have a happy feeling knowing that she is resting in peace where she always wanted to be. Home!"

"You did the most difficult and at the same time unselfish thing a daughter could do, I am sure your mother is bestowing many blessings on you, Sabrina."

Robyn also asked her about her feelings of relocating.

"I realized I have different situations to deal with at the same time, coming to terms with the house Mom left me, and getting closer to my uncle and family. He longed to have his sister back in his life, and for him I represent her, but I never longed for the relatives I didn't know existed.

They are welcomed into my life, I want to see them as much as possible. I love my uncle, we bonded, but I don't have to leave my country, career and friends to nurture our relationship. Honestly, I am not prepared for those kind of family ties."

Luciana shared with Robyn her disappointment with Jonathan and asked for her opinion.

Robyn listened patiently to everything she had to say and responded:

"A happy marriage or partnership is about compromises, both parties give a little and get a little, mostly on smaller issues or differences... I don't believe it is possible compromising on core values. As a matter of fact I know so!

If compromising becomes one sided it is a sacrifice, and sacrifices will bring pain, resentment and the end of love.

Believe me, Luciana, I made that mistake twice, ending in two failed marriages. In the process I lost the relationship with my only son, he had much more in common with his father, my first husband, and didn't support me on the divorce.

Then I married again and divorced again, only to finally learn that it is our similarities that bind us, our commonalities and core values, not our differences as some people tend to believe that opposites attract, maybe initially, but it doesn't last.

If your fiancé valued that for you the commitment of a marriage should start with a wedding with the participation and blessings of both families, that alone should be important to him too."

Sabrina gave them some privacy and went for a run at the beach with Scotty, she missed him, she would love to have him back but she wouldn't take him, he was happy there.

In consideration of Luciana's emotional turmoil, Sabrina did not mention anything about the new man she met in London recently. But in private she told Robyn about Edward.

"I know you don't need my advice on that, Sabrina, but take your time to know him better, you are vulnerable right now. There is a spot in your life to be filled with love. You don't need any heartache."

Both friends returned to Boston on Sunday evening knowing that their lives would take them in a new direction, one way or another.

After the Fourth of July weekend Luciana told her that she had a change of heart. She agreed with Jonathan and they are eloping.

"I canceled the church date and everything else. My mother is teary, but she told me I should do what is best for me."

"That means you are not having a wedding dress, no celebration? We won't see you getting married? Luci, are you happy with your decision?"

"Happy? I don't know… It contradicts what I said before, but I am compromising, that's all."

Sabrina was surprised by Luciana's sudden change of mind but she respected her friend's decision and didn't say anything else. She felt sad for her, there was no happiness in Luci's eyes, she was going through the motions. The fear of losing Jonathan was dominating her rationale.

Sabrina stepped out of the way and only concentrated on her own life, working intensely and communicating often with her English family and almost every day with Edward.

He has been invested in their long distance relationship, and she was longing to see him again.

She reflected, maybe she was attracted to him because he was Welsh and reminded her of what she knew about her father, that he was a kind and gentle man, or maybe not! That made her a little apprehensive.

Just the thought of it gave her a chill running through her spine:

'Am I attracted to a Welsh man, unconsciously trying to make up for the love and attention I did not receive from my father?'

In her next conversation with her uncle he told her:

"With Layla's help I wrote a compelling letter to Nikos, explaining everything that had happened and my reasons, not all justified, for not returning to Greece sooner. I didn't make any excuses for it, told simply the truth, but I emphasized the tremendous joy that I was feeling for knowing about him. I made it clear that I am not approaching him to take the place of his father, but to be his friend and honor the fact that he is the newest Pheris, he represents the family in the most honorable way.

Before I wrote it I researched about the Greek naval force, the 'Hellenic Navy,' and was glad to see that the Aegean Regional Naval Command based in Piraeus, covering the eastern coast of mainland Greece and most of the Aegean Sea and islands' maritime surveillance, coastal defense and the coordination of the Coast Guard, is under Nikos' responsibility!

The port of Piraeus is very close to Athens, which will make my visit easy. I insisted on coming to see him. I hope he is open to that!"

"I hope he is, Uncle Dim! He will be happy to meet you."

Just two months after their return from their trip to Greece, Dimitri told Sabrina exciting news.

"Nikos called me! We had a long and pleasant conversation. He spoke of his surprise in finding out I was alive and his interest in knowing more about me and my family.

He told me about his family, his wife Calla, and sons Alexander and Adrian, and said that his father is and will always be Orion, the one who loved and raised him, but he would like to meet me, the one who gave him his name and his heritage! I was so happy!"

"I'm glad, Uncle Dim. When are you going to meet him?"

"From now until the end of the year Nikos has many commitments, he suggested that I come in the year's beginning. I will for sure! In the meantime we will talk. I am terribly optimistic, I feel we've established a good connection."

Sabrina rejoiced knowing her uncle was motivated with the prospect, a new chapter in his life. A heartwarming feeling!

Luciana was quiet and absent for a couple of weeks, but she finally came around with a totally different attitude.

"Bri, I thought so much and in the end I decided to use the two week vacation I had scheduled for my wedding and honeymoon to go to Portugal alone. Jonathan and I are done!"

She sobbed.

"I am sorry, Luci. What happened?"

"We were having a conversation about the location we were eloping to, Las Vegas or maybe a Caribbean island, when all of a sudden he said that he really didn't care about getting married, he was doing that only because we had dated for five years, and he felt obligated. That hurt me!

Bri, I shouldn't have ignored all the signs of his lack of commitment. I invested five years of my life and love into someone who didn't love me. I can't believe it ended this way!

I finally came to my senses, I am worth more than just settling!"

"You are, Luci, you are! I know things look very bleak right now, but believe me, this shall pass and you'll find happiness. You are being brave standing up for yourself, for your values!"

"Thank you, Bri, for giving me space, you didn't buzz in my

ears what you were feeling or thinking, but I knew, I know you so well. You were disgusted by his behavior, weren't you?"

"And angry, how dare he hurt my best friend! But you are back, Luci, and you'll overcome this. After the storm always comes the sun!"

"I have a new life plan, I might be moving, I already told my parents that when I return from my trip, I am going to explore the possibility of transferring my job and starting my life alone as a mature single woman. Enough of living with Mom and Dad, waiting for the prince to come...

But no matter where I go, they are always going to be my beloved parents and you my best friend-sister! We'll always be together, sharing each others' lives, won't we?"

"We will, Luci, and we'll let life happen!"

The two friends embraced each other and embraced their lives as is.

Weeks later, after Luciana returned in very good spirits, she discussed her plans with her friend.

"Nothing like a change of scenery to put things into perspective! I am optimistic about my future, Bri. I am going to apply for a position at my company's headquarters in New York City, it might take time but I'll get there, I am determined!"

"You are moving on, I am proud of you, Luci! New York is close, we can always be together. I am really happy for you."

"I'll come often to see my parents and you. But I need to ask you, would you keep an eye on my mother? She is being supportive of me, but I know she'll be lonely after I leave."

"Of course, I love Manuela, she has been a force in my life too, she gave me so much care after my Mom was gone. I'll check on her and we might drive together to New York to visit you many times."

"Thank you, Bri. And how is everything with you? Are you planning on leaving your house, or maybe relocating to London?"

"Not right now, Luci, but there is something I didn't tell you because you were going through a rough time... I met someone in London in the summer, we have been in touch, almost daily. It seems to work at a distance and he wants to come to see me here, I'm planning to see him there over the holidays.

And, yes, my uncle would like me to move to England. I was honest and told him I won't make a rushed decision to move, for now I belong here, I am not ready to go anywhere else. But I will someday, life keeps moving forward..."

"I know you won't make a rushed decision, but if you go, there is nothing wrong in having someone there to love and to love you."

"I have a cool head, and I don't know Edward that well, for now it's just a long distance relationship. I need to make a decision not to please anyone, it has to be right for all!"

"You need to make a decision that pleases just one, yourself! And I am glad you met someone, Bri, I hope he is the right one."

"Time will tell, Luci."


In December, Dimitri and Layla were waiting for Sabrina at Heathrow Airport, with joy and hugs.

She immediately noticed a new light in her uncle's eyes, of optimism, of enthusiasm for his newfound family in Greece!

"Because of Nikos I'll be returning to Greece for the second time in less than a year, I won't be alone, Cassius is coming with me!"

They left her at Maurice's apartment before returning to Manchester.


Sabrina finally saw Edward, after so long.

"I am so glad you are here! Our age of social media communication is wonderful, but there is nothing like the personal, face to face contact, the touch, the warmth..."

"I am happy to see you, Edward, there is nothing like being close, you are right."

"I want to see you every day, Sabrina."

"First I am spending Christmas with my uncle and family, then I'll spend a week here in London."

"Where are you staying, with your cousins? Come and stay with me, let's make the best of our time!"


She went to Manchester with Norah, who took her out for some last minute shopping, but most of all she went for her friendly company.

The family home was fully decorated, Sabrina never saw

anything that big and beautiful!

In the presence of the entire family, Dimitri announced:

"Everyone, this is the most joyous event, our Sabrina came home to celebrate our first Christmas together!

I owe to you, Sabrina, all the countless blessings you brought into my life! Because of you, I returned to my roots, I took my sister home, found an unexpected son who carries the family name for generations to come. I'm proud of him, and I am proud of my heritage!"

She received many presents that day, like never before, and so many hugs and kisses from her cousins and spouses, and they all told her the same thing: "We love you, you are part of us!"

Sabrina never felt loved by so many. She had a new feeling of what it was like to belong to a large family that until a year ago she didn't know existed.

That made her think how lonely her life in Boston would be away from them.

Dimitri told her, "Maurice said that there is a certain man in London that is smitten with you. Is he a good reason for you to consider a move?"

"There is a certain Welsh man, we are in a long distance relationship, I like him but he is not the reason for my decision, yet. We need more time to know each other better. I trust life, Uncle Dim, but sometimes people come and go."

"I hope he deserves you, I want to see you happy, my darling niece!"

"I am giving life a chance, Uncle Dimitri. One day at a time!"


Dimitri was enthusiastic telling that he found a Greek lady who is a teacher in town, and she is going to translate Dinora's journals.

"Athena reminded me of my first teacher, Edessa. She will do a great job, she writes really well. When she is finished I decided I will give you the originals, you should have them as Dinora's only heir and the one who fulfilled her last wish. If it weren't for you we would never have gone to Pherula and found her journals."

"Thank you, Uncle Dim, and after we have the translation I might put it all together in a book. As a matter of fact, that is exactly what I will do, adding some of Mom's writings, we will have a book with stories of our family, the Pheris family!"

She was somber for a while, thinking of her Mom…
The family gathered around her. They told her:
"Dinora is here with us in spirit, she is in peace!"

Sabrina went to London and spent days with Edward talking about life and love. She noticed how methodical he was, but very attentive. Her days were warmer in his company, and it was difficult to leave him.

Before their goodbyes he assured her, "I'll see you soon."

She returned to the cold winter and grim month in Boston, when she remembered the anniversary of her Mom's death.

'Two years, so much has happened, but my feelings for her never changed. Love never dies.

I celebrate Mom's life, and thinking of her my heart is full of love. Oh, but I miss her so, it hurts…'

Every time Edward talked to her, she smiled, it made her feel happy! He shared his daily life, his thoughts and feelings with her, and hers with him. By that time she thought she knew him well and she liked him more and more.

She shared with Luciana:

"How crazy is this! I only met him a few times, we talk every day, I can't fall into this trap, I am too lonely."

"Rationalizing your emotions about men was something you always did well, and still sometimes they took the best out of you."

"You are right, Luci, not long ago I believed I was going to marry Tom."

"And I was planning a wedding with Jonathan, and look at us! We never know what is going to happen next."

"The best is yet to come, Luci, life has opened new possibilities for us."

On the eve of Valentine's Day, Edward asked Sabrina to wait at home by 8:00 a.m. for a delivery.

"I didn't think you British men would care much about Valentine's Day!"

"All of a sudden I care! Be there, please!"

She went to bed thinking, 'He is so naïve, but charming. How can I be surprised with a delivery of red roses or chocolates, or maybe both!'

She got up and got ready for work and waited. 8:00, 8:10, 8:20 a.m. went by.
'I am going to be late for work.'
The bell rang, she rushed to the door, all she saw in front of her face was an enormous bouquet of red roses, but behind it, with a big bright smile, "Edward! You are here!"
Her heart fluttered!
"Did I surprise you, Sabrina?"
"Oh my, you did! You are bold, come in!"
He held her tight. "I know how important Valentine's Day is in America, and I flew from London to bring you roses and ask you to be my Valentine. Isn't that how it is done? Is that romantic?"
"Yes, that's very romantic and unexpected, Edward."
He kissed her, they kissed with so much passion. She felt like... She couldn't explain why she was feeling that way.
She asked him, "How long are you staying?"
"I only have until Sunday and I want to spend every minute with you, Sabrina."
"So do I, just us for three entire days. I am going to call in sick, I am not going to work. You are staying here with me, aren't you?"
"Of course, if I am invited."
"You are invited into my house and into my life. Oh, Edward, I am so happy you came!"

And for three days she left her doubts and loneliness behind. She allowed love back into her life, like there was no one else in the world.
They shared every moment of every day and night. He told her he had fallen in love with her when they first met. She told him she was falling in love with him.
During those days he wanted to talk about things that they didn't discuss in emails or phone conversations.
First he offered her information about his family, and why he moved to London.
He said that growing up he didn't have much of his father's presence. His parents divorced when he was a little boy and both

of them remarried and had other children.

He grew up divided between two households, not feeling that he belonged in either one.

"I am sorry, Edward, I had no idea you also came from a broken family, I know how that impacts a child's life. I grew up without my father, not even knowing who he was."

Sabrina told him all the truth about Byron and her mother.

"As you see I am an 'illegitimate love child.' What do you think of that?"

"I think every child should be born out of love! Nothing wrong with it!"

"I am glad you see things this way, with no judgments. And what is the second thing about yourself you want to tell me?"

"I was living with a girl, Janice, for three years, and that relationship ended. Throughout I sensed that our feelings were getting lukewarm, but I thought that was what happens in a long term relationship and I didn't do anything about it. In the end she is the one who left me."

"Why are you telling me this, Edward? Are you still thinking of her? Do you have any unresolved feelings?"

"No, but it is hard to forget I was put down, I never thought she would leave me, and when Janice left she said I was boring. Do you think I am boring, Sabrina?"

"Not so far, on the contrary you seem impetuous. But, you made me a little worried, it looks like she still has an impact on you. Have you seen her recently?"

"That's not it, I haven't seen her in a long time. I was just thinking that I don't want to get into another serious relationship to be put down again."

"Well, I can tell you this, Edward, I would never be in a 'lukewarm' relationship for three years."

He smiled. "Neither would I."

Edward had to leave, he made promises to continue talking every day, and she will see him in London next time.

She was left thinking of that last conversation. 'What was that all about?'

She reflected and realized that the ties she formed with her new family were strong, and she was determined to maintain a lasting relationship with them, even at a distance.

There was also Edward, how would she know if it would work out? 'I'll never know how life would have been if I didn't try.'

She had a heart to heart conversation with Robyn.

"I am still hesitating about considering a transfer to London, I need to be sure. Lately I have been remembering my Mom's words, things that she taught me and now they make much sense to me.

She always said that we should be strong to be able to stand our ground, be true to ourselves, and many times when we make decisions that affect our future led by fear or others' influence we might regret it to the end of our days. 'Regret is like a burning hole in our hearts that never heals!'"

"That's wise! It sounds like Blythe's words, now we know quite well why she felt that way. But do not let a day go by in your life that you don't live the way you are supposed to. Bri, conquer your destiny.

I heard these words from your mother in the past when I was at an impasse of a major decision. I am sure she would repeat them to you now."

"She would, I can hear my Mom's voice in your voice. I need to be honest and tell you that everybody thinks I am self assured and fearless, that's not true, Ma Robyn! I am afraid of making a mistake. Like everyone else I am scared of putting myself in situations that would result in disappointment."

"Bri, you are strong and wise beyond your years. You'll make the right decision, and everything will be alright!"

"Thank you, Ma Robyn, talking to you is like speaking to my Mom!"

Sabrina didn't feel anxious, from then on she remained true to herself and her feelings.

She became absolutely sure that there would be light coming through the mist of her doubts, and deep inside she knew she would do what was right.

After months of interviews and going back and forth to New York, Luciana found the perfect position in her company.

"I'll be moving next month, Bri, my office building is on Third Avenue and I found a co-worker who lives a few blocks away and needs a roommate. Would you help me move? I am so anxious!"

"I am happy for you, Luci! Your life is opening up, you made it happen! And of course I will help, let's have a moving marathon, your parents and I will bring you to New York City!"

"I am a little afraid, Bri, do you think I am capable of living alone?"

"Of course! You are going to have a brand new life and you won't be far from Boston at all."

"I wish you would come too, Bri. Will you come to visit me often?"

"We don't know what life has in store for us, Luci. No matter how far we are, I will always come to see you."

Edward and Sabrina continued talking every day. She had been a little evasive in their conversations and he perceived it as being cold.

He told her he was coming to see her again soon. She asked him to wait until her vacation was confirmed, when she was planning to see him in London.

"I miss you, Sabrina, it looks like you don't miss me as much as I do."

"You are wrong, Edward, I miss you too! I can't wait to see you again."

"Why don't you want me to come?"

"Because I am tied up at work and still debating with myself about moving to London or not. Please understand that would be the most important decision of my life so far.

I want you to know that I am not putting any pressure on you, Edward, although I want our relationship to grow I won't do it just for that reason."

"I understand, you are being very sensible about us, Sabrina. I am in love with you, and I want us to be together!"

"I want the same and I truly believe that if we are meant to be together it will happen, Edward, life has its ways!"

# CHAPTER EIGHT

# NEW BEGINNINGS

$S$abrina had a conversation with her boss, explaining that for family reasons she has been contemplating the idea of moving to London.

At that point all she wanted was to inquire about the possibility of a transfer, to continue working with the firm if she decided to relocate.

"When you have the time I would like to discuss it. I am only exploring, there is nothing decided right now, but to come to a final resolution I need to put all the pieces together."

Wyatt was taken by surprise.

He told her she was a great asset for the firm and they didn't want to lose her. He seemed rushed and didn't have much time to talk to her or to confirm her next vacations, as she requested. He said they should talk about it later.

"Maybe we will go out for a drink together, after work."

"I'd suggest coffee right here in your office, Wyatt!"

He was in a hurry for a court appearance and left.

Sabrina has worked with Wyatt for seven years, since her days as an intern. So far he has been a supportive mentor and also a friend.

More often than not, during her career she would stay late to discuss work matters with him after hours.

At the end of the day he was not back, she went home.

The next day Wyatt called Sabrina to his office and gave her a new assignment, a complex case.

"I came back late yesterday but you had left, Sabrina. Anyway it's about this new assignment, you are the right one to take care of this, it's a big responsibility, we will be working on it together.

Regarding your vacations, sorry I can't confirm anytime soon, maybe you can take a long weekend here and there, until you complete this project.

Please come back to my office by the end of the day, we'll talk."

She returned to his office later.

He offered her some scotch.

"Thanks, Wyatt, but I don't drink. What do you want to talk about?"

"I want to ask you if you are seriously thinking about moving to London."

"Just thinking… My relatives keep insisting that I join them, they are great people and it would be nice to be close to them, especially now that I don't have any family left here."

"To be honest, Sabrina, I don't want you to go. I would like you to stay here with us, you are up for a promotion, pretty soon you might become a partner in the firm, it all depends on you!"

"A partner? I hadn't thought of that. That's why you entrusted me with that demanding case?"

"I entrusted it to you because I know you are perfectly capable of executing it, and also because I want us to work closer and spend more time together. Sabrina, don't you understand what I am trying to say?

The truth is I am very attracted to you, I am certain we can be very successful together."

"Wyatt, what are you talking about? I am feeling uncomfortable with this conversation. Where are you going with this?"

"Have you been oblivious? I already told you, Sabrina, I am attracted to you, I was giving you some time to come to terms after your loss, but now that I see you upbeat, strong, going on with your life I thought there is a possibility for us to be together."

Sabrina was taken by surprise with his words and intentions, but she kept calm and composed.

"Wyatt, throughout all of these years I have respected you, relied on you as my mentor, we have worked together really well, I have considered you a friend, and that's all there is. Are you forgetting you are married? Why do you think I would consider this kind of relationship with you?"

"My marriage is over, it's in shambles, I am done with it and I want a new life with someone who I have more in common with, another legal mind, but most of all someone I love and desire."

"That's not me. Maybe the only thing we do have in common is as you said 'our legal minds,' I am going to forget you told me this, maybe you are under the effect of the scotch. I am going home, you should do the same. Goodnight, Wyatt."

He made an attempt to approach her. She quickly stepped away.

She was shaking when she left the office. In that environment she had learned much, grown professionally, made a few friends, all of that was shattered by his action.

'He might come to his senses and apologize tomorrow. I'll let it go, for now.'

She hadn't seen Shelton in a while. He came to visit her.

"The other day Robyn and I were talking about you, and she said that you were still considering moving to England. She knows you are going to do the wisest thing, but if you go, Sabrina, I would miss you. I think of you like if you were my daughter."

"I'd miss you too, Shelton, you were the only father figure I had, you will always be part of my life, for that reason I want to tell you something I haven't shared with anyone yet, I have this gut feeling that keeps telling me, 'Don't go, it's not the right time!'"

"Is that about the boyfriend? Are you sure about that relationship?"

"I am quite sure it won't last if it remains distant, our real day to day relationship didn't start yet, let's see what happens."

"Well, I promise I will come to your wedding."

"Wedding? I am not thinking that far! You might have to wait too long."

"Let me tell you how proud I am of you, Sabrina, I trust your judgment, at this point I feel that you already know what to decide, you don't need my advice."

"Thank you, Shelton, for the boost of confidence. But what about you? How have you been?"

"If you are asking about my heartache, it's getting better. I still miss your Mom, but I am going on with my life. I am making a decision about my retirement and I might move to Cape Cod. Robyn is a good motivator and dear friend, like you I have a decision to make."

"Shelton, for all I know, you have been unselfish, putting others' interests ahead of yours. This is your time, think of yourself! Be happy!"

Sabrina trusted and respected him, but she didn't mention the impasse she was having at work with Wyatt. She knew Shelton would be concerned about her, and she didn't want to spoil his visit.

She avoided talking to Wyatt for the next days, but he still approached her, inviting her out for dinner to continue their conversation. She declined every time, asking him to stop.

She was feeling uncomfortable around him.

Luciana called:

"You sound good, Luci, tell me all, how is everything in New York City?"

"It is a big adjustment, but I am doing fine, the only thing I don't like much is the roommate situation. To live here is so expensive, I can't afford to be on my own for now. But the social life is great! Happy hours almost every night after work, meeting people, and men, many men…"

"Anyone in particular?"

"Not yet, they come and go, but I am working on it. I do not want to be an old spinster!"

"Spinster? Such an old word! Oh, Luci, I have been upset about something that is happening at work, I wish I could talk to you."

"What are you doing this weekend, Bri? Come, we will have fun, and you will take your mind off it."

"I'll do that, I need a breather."

Sabrina went to spend the weekend with Luciana and told her all about Wyatt's unwanted advances.

"Look at this situation, it added one more problem for me to solve. I am really upset, the feeling that I had for my job and my workplace has been tainted."

"That is ridiculous! Was he drunk? Are you thinking of leaving your job? What about Edward? Do you see a future with him?"

"I don't know what the future reserves for us, right now it is fine just the way it is. Let's see where it takes us…"

"I agree with you, Bri, you have much to think about!"

The weekend in New York City was relaxing.

Luciana was unstoppable, she had activities all planned out, day and night, walking in the Park, shopping, going out for dinner, dancing.

"Let's go out to meet people! I am recovering from all the five years lost in that failed relationship when I sat at home waiting for 'Mr. Right' to show up on his time."

"Luci, it is nice to see you so motivated and upbeat, but please don't burn out."

"Life is short, Bri, I am thirty years old and I have no time to waste."

"We are both thirty, and I feel that life is just starting, but I agree we shouldn't waste any time. Time is all we have!"

"Now that you are not happy with your job anymore, and you are not sure about moving to London, would you consider coming to New York? Can you imagine how much better it would be if you were here too?"

"I didn't think of that until this moment. That is something to consider… Maybe a new job in New York City!"

Sabrina went home resolute and organized her thoughts.

'For over two years I have been living in emotional turmoil and conflict, dealing with grief, followed by the discovery about Mom's life, about my father, finding my uncle, the heart-wrenching trip to Greece, a new love, and now an issue with my job.

My life needs a complete overhaul.

Should I leave everything and move to London? Starting over in a new country, that's what my Mom did when she was at an impasse.

Time to take action!'

Dimitri returned from his trip to Greece and called his niece. He was euphoric!

"The whole experience was amazing, I am glad Cassius came to support me. We went to meet Nikos at the Naval Command, it was a great introduction and I had the shock of my life when 'Captain Pheris' came out of his office, he was the spitting image of my father.

In his impressive uniform and with a welcoming smile, and hearing him describe his love for the sea and his passion for his career, I thought of my father who was also 'a man of the sea,' but let his passion be trampled by his ambition."

"Tell me all, Uncle Dim, did you meet his family? Did he get along with Cassius?"

"Yes, I met his wife Calla, a beautiful woman, kind and generous, she sent presents to all the children in our family in England.

And my teenage grandsons, Alexander and Adrian, they have the same posture as their father. The best of all is that they started calling me grandfather right away, I am now their Pappous!

With Nikos, we spent a few days going around, we saw everything in the town of Piraeus, and in the port we visited some of the Navy ships, but most of all Nikos and I talked quite a lot about everything, my relationship with his mother... I can say that we became friends. Cassius and Nikos got along really well, like two good brothers."

"Uncle Dim, you deserve this amazing gift that life brought you, after so many decades of hurt and doubts, here came the light, in the form of a bright naval commander, your son!"

"Light and redemption, Sabrina. Redemption for my father's deeds, and in the process I'm redeemed too. As I embraced my new son I forgave my father, in my heart there is no more anger or hatred.

The Pheris family lives on and will continue with Nikos and his sons. I am proud of my Greek family!"

"It all happened like a miracle! I want to believe that was my Mom's doing, you brought her home and in return you found your peace!"

Edward and Sabrina continued their conversations. But talking was not enough for them, they longed for one another.

He asked her when she was coming back to London.

"I am tied up at work, a demanding project, they postponed my vacations, maybe if I am lucky I'll come in the fall, if not I'll come by the end of the year. I promised Uncle Dimitri that I'll be there for the holidays again."

"The holidays? I can't wait six months to see you. I am coming, maybe you can take me to the beach for a few days."

"I'd love it if you come, Edward, and I'll take you to a very special beach town."

She called her godmother.

"Ma Robyn, Edward is coming, I am getting deeper and deeper into this relationship. Would you like to meet him?"

"Absolutely, darling, I'd love to meet him, bring him for a weekend. Hopefully Shelton will be here too and we can all get acquainted."

Edward came! Her heart was full of joy.

She showed him two rooms in her house, now empty, that he didn't see before.

"I am painting them, I am getting the house ready to rent. I don't want to sell it yet, but I have decided, I'm moving out."

"I agree, this house is too large for you alone."

"I have emotional ties with my house, more than that it holds many memories… It hurts to leave, but it hurts more to stay. I still have a few more things to do before I lease it."

"Are you planning to continue living in Boston? Did you make a decision about moving away?"

"I love my country, my city. I am trying to be true to myself, I have doubts, and my inner voice tells me no! I don't feel that I should move far away right now.

Please understand, Edward, it is not that I don't want to be with you. But I don't want to move either. My decision has been made."

She felt an enormous relief saying it out loud.

"Did you tell your uncle?"

"I have told him I was not ready for a decision. I'm planning to tell him in person by the holidays."

"He will understand."

"I am counting on that, I don't want to hurt him or you, for that matter."

"I have thought about it, Sabrina, in case you decide not to come to London I would consider coming to the United States temporarily, to be with you and to make our relationship grow."

"Are you serious, Edward? I have to tell you that I had thought of moving there because of you. When I told you it was only about my family it was not quite true, I have to confess that it scared me to think that I would change my life and then things wouldn't work for us."

"It is the same distance for you to move there or for me to move here.

Sabrina, I need to ask you, would you live with me? I am not coming to be alone, I want us to be together."

"All of a sudden I see a new possibility for us and I like it, Edward. I had thought, why am I the one that has to move? Our relationship should be equally important for both of us.

Yes, of course, I will be with you. I am at the point to say that I want to see our relationship grow. But wouldn't you miss England, London?"

"Probably, I have lived there for half of my life. I am adaptable and that's all I needed to hear, my love.

Don't be in a hurry to find another place, we might do it together. The other day there was a conversation in my company about a project in the United States. All I can say now is I'll be looking into the possibilities."

Sabrina's heart exploded with certainty, she felt she had found the right man to love and to hold, and he is coming into her life at the right time.

She took Edward to Cape Cod to enjoy the weekend at the beach, but mostly to meet Robyn and Shelton.

"Robyn is my godmother and Shelton, my father figure, he was Mom's boyfriend since I was ten years old. I love them both and they are anxious to meet you."

"So, it will be like meeting your parents?"

"Sort of, they are as close to real family as they could be."

The days in Cape Cod were delightful. The weather was most pleasant, and Robyn and Shelton were interested in getting to know Edward.

He was a little reserved, but very agreeable with both of them.

Before returning she told them she would call them to know their opinion about Edward.

"I respect your opinion, please tell me your impressions of him, and what you think of both of us together."

After a couple of days in Boston with her, Edward left, promising they would be together soon.

She called her godmother.

"Please tell me, Ma Robyn, what are your thoughts and impressions of Edward?"

"After you left, Shelton and I discussed it, we both had the same good impression, he is polite, reserved, maybe it is a British thing, he looked very controlled, not revealing emotions, maybe a little aloof. Do you know what I mean?"

"They call it the 'stiff upper lip.' You are right about that, but he is serious about us and committed to our relationship."

"And you look good together, Bri!"

"Well, he said there is a possibility that he would come here to be with me. I am thinking seriously about it. How would I know if he is the right one if I don't spend more time with him?"

"I agree with that, if you have that opportunity it would be ideal, I would not rush into marriage knowing him, or anyone else, for a short period of time, and I really don't trust long distance relationships. I can add that Shelton feels the same way."

"Thank you, Ma Robyn, you know how much I value your opinion, the same way as I respected Mom's. You are my second mother."

"I am your godmother, that's my role now. I am here for you, Bri, whenever you need me, in any circumstance."

She talked to Luciana.

"Listen, sister, I made two major decisions. I can't come to terms with selling my house, but I'll be renting it, and I am not moving to London!"

"I am so happy! Where are you moving to?"

"I was planning on renting an apartment in downtown Boston, and looking for another job in the city, or maybe even exploring New York City, but I put that plan on hold for now.

Edward might come to the States temporarily, and we will move in together. That's when I am going to look for a new job!"

"Amazing, your life is coming together, this is exciting news! When is Edward coming? For how long?"

"I don't know yet, he told me there is something in the works in his company. He will know soon.

What about you, Luci, meet anyone special?"

"Oh, Bri, every day I meet someone special, but they are just passing by."

"You make me laugh, Luci. When you least expect it, one of these days you'll find him, the one, Mr. Right."

"Is Edward your Mr. Right?"

"I want him to be, but I do not know yet!"

"Tell me, Bri, how is your boss behaving lately?"

"The same, he has made some inappropriate comments, and I keep putting him off. He doesn't see it coming, I am ready to leave, I already did a little research on other law firms!

I'm looking forward to finish my last assignment, get a good recommendation and leave."

A month later, Edward announced:
"I am coming for a meeting and I would like you to come with me. It's a project on Connecticut's coast, Bridgeport, just like one I designed here. I hear that it is the largest town in that state, and it is in the New England area, as you like it.
Initially it would be a year contract with my company's new American merger. The corporate office building is in White Plains, Westchester County, New York. Do you know the area?"
"I do, it is north of New York City. And, yes, I'll come with you, I'll arrange a couple of days off, we can drive, it is only about two hours from here."

Edward arrived and together with Sabrina went on a road trip.
He told her:
"They are developing a waterfront project with plans to build in other areas of the East Coast. I already met the project investor in London.
I want to see if I like White Plains, where I'll be based. You'll need to compromise, Sabrina, I am afraid you have to leave your job to move in with me."
"It is all so sudden, Edward, if you are willing to relocate, I am willing to leave Boston. To tell you the truth I was going to change jobs anyway. When are you coming?"
"In January, we have a couple of months to make the arrangements, find a place to start our new life together."
"I will be coming to London for the holidays and I want to bring you to Manchester to meet my uncle, we will tell him about us."
"I agree, I wish I could bring you to my family, but I don't believe they care at all about what I am doing or where I am going.
Someday we might go together to Wales, I'll show you around, after all it is your country too."
"It is, I would love to visit it with you! Edward, what is going to happen after one year? Would you have to return to London?"
"To be honest I do not intend to move permanently, but it might be necessary to extend my contract in the States, or we might

return together to England as a married couple! I really don't know. Anything is possible!"

"Thank you for being honest with me, Edward, I am happy that you are coming, I am ready to take our first big step towards our life together!"

She was left with the task of finding an apartment in White Plains.

She told Luciana that in the meantime she had to forgo her job, rent her house, look for another job, and go to London by the end of the year.

"Bri, I can't contain myself, please, please look for a job here in Manhattan, you can easily commute, thousands of people do that every day, the train from White Plains to Grand Central only takes about thirty minutes. And I will see you often."

"I'll try, Luci, I really want a change, I'd like to find a more meaningful job, I am tired of dealing with business law and contracts. As soon as I am done with the case I am working on, I will resign. I need time to find an apartment and rent my house. Oh, so much to do!"

"I can come with you to help search for an apartment, if you want."

"Of course I want, we will do that, Luci."

Sabrina went across the street to see Manuela and told her what was going to happen.

"Don't be sad, I will see you, and we can meet in Manhattan when you come to see Luci, every time."

"I'll miss you, Sabrina. You are like my second daughter.

When you are ready to rent your house, let me know, I have a friend who is looking for a house for her son and family. They love this area!

You might not need a realtor to help you with that and I'll have some nice neighbors again!"

"You'll be the first to know, Manuela."

The last time Sabrina spoke to her cousin, Norah told her that she was looking forward to see her around the holidays and they might have an engagement party to attend.

Norah and Geoffrey are serious and they are moving together to Birmingham, in the heart of England.

"Great news, Norah, congratulations! How does Uncle Dimitri feel about your move?"

"Dad, my Daddy! He is very supportive, all he wants is to see me happy. The same goes for you, Sabrina, he wants to see you happy!"

"Norah, I also made a final decision, I am not going to move to London, Edward is coming to the United States temporarily, and we will see what happens with us after that..."

"I knew you were going to make the right decision, good luck with your Englishman, he is proving that he is invested in you."

Upon finishing her work assignment she gave her firm two weeks' notice.

"Thank you, Wyatt, you have been a mentor and I have learned quite a lot from you. I have been here for eight years, it is time to move on, I'll miss the firm and the friends I made here.

But I won't go without telling you that your most recent misbehavior, the harassment, tarnished the good experience I had of working with you, and that is when I made the decision to leave."

"I am sorry, Sabrina, I didn't intend to offend you, I truly like you, and I am sad you are leaving us. Are you moving to London?"

"No, I am going to New York."

"I apologize if I made you feel uncomfortable, that was not harassment, I meant what I said, I have true feelings for you.

During the time you were vulnerable, dealing with your loss, I wanted to take you in my arms and tell you how much I cared, I wanted to help you and admired you even more, your strength, your character, your professional skills.

Sabrina, I'll miss you. The door is open, if you decide to come back to Boston you have a place here with us."

"Thank you for your words, Wyatt, that was a clear misstep but I'll remember your guidance and your good deeds.

I wish you the best in your personal and professional life."

Her office offered her a farewell party. She felt truly sad in leaving her colleagues after so many years of collaboration and friendship.

During the month of November, she went to White Plains a few times and found the ideal apartment for her and Edward exactly in the location that he wanted, as close as possible to his office, as he repeatedly reminded her. Luckily it was not far from a train station to make her commute to Manhattan easier.

With Luciana's help she decorated it with most of her own furniture, and rented her house in Beacon Hill to the family that Manuela had introduced to her, a couple with a little boy.
"He will grow up happy here, I did!"

She spent her last day on Wetherill Place at Luciana's parents' house.
She had a knot in her throat.
Manuela hugged her.
"I feel like crying too, it is like losing another daughter."
"You are not losing me, I'll be close and I'll see you here or in New York when you come to see Luci."
Sabrina looked across the street to her house.
"I was just a little girl the first time Mom showed me this street and pointed out that red door, I ran to it, shouting, 'Our house is so beautiful, Mommy!'
It was not only a house like any other on the street, it was my home, and for twenty years the place that I treasured, where there was growth, joy and love, much love, but now it became sad to be there without her, it is time to let go…"
"It is still your house, Sabrina, maybe someday you'll come back!"
"Anything is possible! Mom always wanted to go back home, and she did in the end."

Manuela embraced her and they cried together. It was painful to say goodbye to many years of true friendship, of warmth and solidarity in that lovely neighborhood.
"I'm leaving a piece of my heart here…"

The next day she moved to Westchester County and immediately started interviewing for jobs in Manhattan, where she met Luciana every day.

"I am so happy you came, Bri. We are close again! You will find a job soon, the possibilities are endless here!"

"Yes, Luci, I am trying to get something lined up before I go to London for the holidays.

Life with all the new possibilities, it's beautiful! I found love, you'll find yours, and we are both embarking on this new adventure with confidence."

"Do you feel scared that things might not work out with Edward? Or that you'll miss Boston?"

"I miss Boston already. And, no, I am not scared, I am excited and trust that I can handle what is to come."

"You are so confident, Bri. Nothing seems to faze you, you keep going strong and believing that everything will be alright."

"I survived the worst that could happen, Luci, with you at my side. Our lives are running parallel since we were nine years old, and it will be on and on, for a long time.

Yes, everything will be alright!"

She called Robyn.

"I won't be far, I'll see you as much as before. I'll be talking to you, Ma Robyn, you are the first person I call when I need words of wisdom."

"I'll always be here for you, darling, I am happy you are moving on with your life."

Sabrina went to London in mid-December to spend more time with her uncle, aunt, cousins and their children. She loved how the youngsters call her 'Aunt.'

"I came to stay longer with you and your family, Uncle Dimitri. I'll be starting a new job at the beginning of the year. It is an interesting job, but right now I don't know exactly how busy I am going to be and when I'll be able to come to see you again. Anyway I'll try my best to be here for the holidays every year."

"Sabrina, I am so glad you are here with us, you bring joy into my life, and every time you smile I see my sister smiling at me with those cute little dimples.

I am so grateful that life gave us this chance. I have a heartwarming memory of our adventure in Greece, our village, that will last a lifetime."

"So do I, Uncle Dim, I am happy we went together and we bonded on our spiritual journey!"

"I can only compare the bond that I have with you with the one I had with my sister. Talking about her, I have a very special present for you."

He gave her a box, beautifully wrapped up. She opened it.

"Mom's Greek journals!"

They were individually wrapped in a delicate cloth.

"That's to preserve them. They are rightfully yours, Sabrina. Take a look at the translation, Athena did a wonderful job."

There was a stack of papers in the bottom of the box. She started looking through them.

"Thank you, Uncle Dim, this is the most amazing gift you could ever give me."

They were both emotional. He told her to read the last page.

"Dinora wrote it in 1974, the last time we were in Pherula.

I clearly remember she asked our mother to keep the journals safe from the hands of the children. She said:

*'They need to be preserved, Mama, they tell the history of our family.'"*

Sabrina read the last page:

*'And the summer came to an end, Dimitri and I are returning to school in London, the majestic, wonderful city of palaces, rich in culture, arts and history.*

*But no matter what I experience, learn and see out there in the world my deepest desire is to return to my roots, to this most beloved place on earth. And, right here, contemplating the endless views of the sea, I know, I feel it in my soul, this is where I belong.*

*In every moment, even at a distance, my love for my family and our little village beats to the rhythm of my heart:*

*I'll be back! I'll be back! I'll be back home!'*

Dimitri and Sabrina were melancholic. Tears were streaming down their faces.

"We did it, Uncle Dim! We brought her home, we fulfilled Mom's wish, but it is so sad, her eyes never saw that view again, her heart didn't experience the joy of returning."

"Her soul rejoiced! She was united with our family where she always wanted to be. We shall find comfort in that."

"Uncle Dim, I am going to have it printed in a book and each one of our family and best friends will have a copy.

I will write an epilogue telling the story will continue with Nikos. He is like a phoenix that came out of the ashes of destruction to continue the heritage of hard working and dignified men that built their own village out of a pile of rocks and stones with their bare hands, and generation after generation they loved their village, its fertile soil and the sea. With Nikos and his two boys the Pheris family legacy will go on and on...

That will be my gift to our family, for the ones here now and for generations to come."

"Magnificent, darling! Well said!"

"It will be the only book authored by Dinora Pheris, the most precious one of all, and also my homage and great respect for my Mom's life!

I personally know a publisher in Boston, the one who worked with her, printing her books and essays as Dr. Blythe Lisvane."

Sabrina leaned her head on his shoulder.

"Oh, Uncle Dim, I love my Mom forever and ever... And I love you and our family."

He embraced her.

"My little one, I love you!"

They stayed in silence for a while.

Later...

"New life, Sabrina, new life! Tell me, when am I meeting Edward? Is he coming to Manchester?"

"Yes, Uncle Dim, he will come to meet you next week, he is getting ready with his apartment and belongings, to return with me to New York on the first day of January. I am quite sure you'll like him."

"If you like him, I'll probably like him too. Are you planning on marrying him?"

"I have been thinking about it, I am in love with him and very optimistic about us. Edward and I have reasonable expectations and we are both willing to invest in our relationship. Still I'll take my time to know him better to be able to make the best decision.

The day I marry it will be with absolute certainty that I found my true, everlasting companion to build a family together. I take marriage very seriously."

"As you should, Sabrina! I completely trust your judgment, but I have questions for him, and also recommendations. I want to tell Edward that you had your share of suffering and you deserve happiness. I expect him to be kind and supportive of you and give you the best life possible.

I know you are resilient and capable, but it is a fact of life that hardships and challenges are unavoidable, and I need the reassurance that he will stand with you through it all."

"You sound like a concerned father, Uncle Dim. I appreciate that you care and I count on you. I am not alone, I have you here 'across the pond,' just a few hours away.

I do not expect to have my heart broken ever again, but if it happens I know I will get up and continue living. I am ready for this new chapter of my life and prepared to accept and embrace whatever will come.

Who would have thought that my life would have changed so dramatically these last years?

Everything seemed stable, uneventful until Mom was gone... My world was shattered, but with that overwhelming devastation I was awakened to a new life of discoveries, showing me new nuances, possibilities, it taught me I needed to do some groundbreaking work to transcend any limitation I had, whether it was of pain or fear.

I also learned that life is ever changing with unexpected events and unforeseen consequences, some devastating, others simply blissful, and through our struggles we gain the ability to cope and see the light!"

"I'm proud of you, Sabrina, I wish you much happiness, and in my heart I still hope that you will join us someday. But always remember, no matter how far, as long as I live I am here supporting you."

"Thank you, Uncle Dim. Perhaps these are the right circumstances that will bring us close together, united in one big family here in England.

I am optimistic, I've always believed things will happen when they are meant to be… There is a reason for everything. As my Mom used to say, *'It is all written in the stars!'*"

The Thanov family holiday celebration was warm and filled with joy, as always. Uncle Dimitri was very happy.

"Our family is growing, Norah and Geoffrey are getting married soon, and we now welcome Edward!"

They liked him and agreed he was a good fit for Sabrina, he was very caring towards her, everyone could see they were in love.

Dimitri told his niece: "I am hopeful that one year from now we will have another wedding announcement…"

Sabrina and Edward returned together to New York. As they settled in their apartment in White Plains, she told him how excited she was about her new job in Manhattan.

"It's a dream job!"

To her surprise, Edward was unappreciative.

"But you have to commute to the city every day, isn't that too much?"

"Not really, thousands of people do it. The train from here to Grand Central Station takes about thirty minutes, and I have the option of working from home on days that I am researching, isn't that great?"

He frowned.

"Why, Edward, don't you think it's a good idea?"

"You should have a job around this area, Sabrina, it is only for a year, then we will be returning to England."

"We might, we don't know what is going to happen in the future, right now I am interested in learning all about my new job, and there is one more thing, I'll be taking German classes!"

"German? Is that a requirement?"

"No, but it helps with the job and it never hurts to learn another language, especially in my profession. They were very accommodating, I will take the classes during my work hours."

"What about us? Are you going to have time for us?"

"Of course, Edward, our relationship is my priority. You have your job, I have mine, we are like any other working couple."

She hugged and kissed him.

"Don't worry, we'll have plenty of time to be together."

Although they were starting the phase when everything should have been about togetherness and love, Sabrina was making an effort to enjoy his company and get used to his particular habits.

Edward was settled in his own ways, not easily adaptable to the new environment and often preoccupied with what was not important.

She was being patient, but started feeling uneasy. Her job became a sore point in their conversation, for him there was no reason for her 'to waste her time in a job that she would be leaving soon.'

Edward was a homebody, expecting her to be at his side all the time. As far as she was at home with him, sitting on the same sofa, watching a movie on TV, he was content!

Her attempts to talk to him about improving their relationship were disregarded. There was much she wanted to share with him, experiences, feelings and thoughts. She told him that they used to talk much more about themselves online before, what was happening now? He would respond that he was happy just being close to her!

Sometimes on weekends she suggested they go to the city, to a restaurant, a theater or a concert. He would make excuses, saying he was tired and always questioned her. "You go to the city every day, just relax."

More often than she wanted to hear, he stated that he didn't like New York City or the American lifestyle.

His conversations were superficial and dull. He complained often about small or unimportant things: "There are no pubs here." "I can't find my favorite beer." "I hate the traffic, the supermarket, the stores." "The streets are crowded with noisy people."

During the summer, after she insisted, Edward agreed in going to Cape Cod to visit Robyn and Shelton only once.
"Let's go, Edward, don't you enjoy going to the beach? It is so pleasant there, and I miss Ma Robyn and Shelton, they are more than friends, they filled the void that my blood relatives, for whatever circumstance, were not able to. I love them!"

Once there, Edward was polite with them, but he wouldn't leave Sabrina alone, whether inside the house or at the beach.

In a rare moment when he was sitting on the patio, having a drink with Shelton, her godmother commented:
"It looks like Edward is very attached to you, Sabrina, but you don't seem happy. What is going on?"
"He is clinging but that doesn't mean I feel loved! Six months into our relationship and he keeps complaining every day that I spend too much time talking to Luciana or that I leave work late. He is not being reasonable, I only meet Luci at lunchtime, and many days I leave work hurried and anxious to get to the train station on time.
He has rules, he wants me home ready for dinner at seven o'clock, he is so particular. Sometimes I feel suffocated!
I am dealing with an inflexible man, not willing to compromise. To tell you the truth, Ma Robyn, I am disappointed, he seemed upbeat before, and now everything became a challenge for him. He has a hard time adapting to new life circumstances."
"What is wrong with him? Does he regret being here? It is only for a year, he should make the best out of it!"
"I know! He keeps saying he misses London. When we were there last month for Norah's wedding, he complained too because we had to stay at my cousins'. His apartment was not available, he sublet it when he came.
I am going to see my uncle and family at the end of the year, and he is already complaining he doesn't have his own place.
I have tried to talk about how I am feeling, so many times. It's frustrating!"
"Bri, what else is wrong? I know you, I am not seeing any enthusiasm, are your feelings for Edward fading away?"

"I am sad, I am starting to admit that we are a mismatch, everything was great at a distance, I am afraid the passion that brought us together is gone."

"Do you regret leaving Boston for him?"

"I do not, Ma Robyn. He is not responsible for it, I needed a change and I would never know what the future reserved for us if I hadn't taken the chance. Being in New York is fantastic, I am close to my friend, and I have a great job in Manhattan!"

"You are excited about your job. Tell me more about it."

"It's meaningful, the kind of work that demands much learning and research about a time in history that impacted so many lives during World War II, in several countries in Europe. It's a work of the heart!

I never knew that my international law skills would be well applied to it."

"It's nice to see how enthusiastic you are about it, Bri. Do you think it would be a consideration to leave your job to continue the relationship with Edward, eventually moving to London with him?"

"I didn't think that far and didn't lose hope yet, things might improve with Edward, maybe he just needs more time to adapt."

"Some people do, some others never adapt to a shared life. It is not fair that you would have to mold your life to conform to his ways."

"It wouldn't be fair, but I'll give us some more time... That's why we decided to live together, to know each other better. Wasn't it?"

"You don't need my advice, Bri, you are sensible, you will know what to do."

"What about you and Shelton, Ma Robyn? He was saying that he is finally retiring and will be spending most of his time here at the Cape. Are you in a romantic relationship?"

"No, Bri, it's not romantic. For both of us, at our age, we are very happy to share a solid and meaningful friendship. Shelton is an exceptional man, and I love to have him in my life."

"He is exceptional, so are you, Ma Robyn, and I wish happiness to both of you! Sometimes we don't need 'romance' in our lives, we need a trustworthy, loving friend as our companion to feel loved and supported.

Right now I am not feeling either, and the romance is going out the window…"

Despite Sabrina's willingness and efforts, months went on and things did not change, it became a constant struggle for her to keep being positive and hopeful, trying to make it work.

Edward was a man of few words and didn't believe that their relationship needed any attention.

She reflected on the times they spent before they moved in together. They were far in between occasions, just for a few days, either in Boston or London.

During those days they would stay home, 'making up for the time when they were apart.' She observed him being very methodical and there was no initiative on his part to share or create new experiences for them.

She came to realize he would never change, that was his nature, being unappreciative of what he had.

For Edward, just being physically around her was enough.

She remembered that once he commented that his previous girlfriend had left him, claiming that he was 'boring.'

'Now I know!'

Sabrina discussed with him that she was not feeling validated and was broken-hearted seeing their connection fading away…

She took upon herself the responsibility to improve their life together and asked him what she could do.

Again, it seemed he made a deaf ear or he was just oblivious, settled in his own ways. He didn't see the need to make an effort.

At that point she realized that she was the only one invested in their relationship.

Getting closer to the end of his contract, Edward was offered an option to stay another year in New York or return to London with the prospect of a promotion.

"What did you decide, Edward?"

"I want to go back to London as soon as possible with you, Sabrina, I want you to be my wife, we should get married."

"Married? Edward, I appreciate the fact that you care about me, but this year together has proved to both of us that we have different values and expectations about constructing a life together. I don't believe that marriage would work for us."

"I thought you were happy, Sabrina. Wasn't it enough that I left everything in London to be with you? What happened?"

"What didn't happen? That's the question. What went missing? I would say it was the lack of warmth, open communication to understand each other's needs, sharing our feelings, ideas and goals.

Edward, I told you on many occasions I didn't feel like your partner or companion, I felt like I was your mother taking care of everything around here, making your life comfortable, motivating you!

We have very different expectations, Edward. We would not be a happy couple. If I am not happy, how could you be?"

"I didn't know you felt this way, Sabrina, I really believed we were perfect for each other. You are attentive and caring, I feel good around you, I love you."

"I love you too, Edward, you are a good man, I know you didn't intend to hurt me, I don't want to hurt you either, but we need to be realistic. I am sorry, we are not right for each other."

"If I knew that this year would end this way with me returning alone, I would not have made the sacrifice of coming to the U.S."

"Sacrifice? I thought you did it with an open heart for us, for yourself, for your career! Remember I also made changes in my life because I believed in us and wanted to give us the opportunity to make our relationship flourish.

I am heartbroken, Edward, it does hurt to see you go, to let go of the dream that we could have a real, happy marriage."

"You might regret it, Sabrina. When you come to London, let me know if you have changed your mind. We can still be together, I am accustomed to you, I'll miss you!"

Sabrina had confided in Luciana many times about how frustrated she was with her relationship with Edward.

"Luci, after he said that word, there was nothing else to be discussed. Accustomed! It's exactly how he feels about me, about us, therefore we should be married! Not that he loved me or couldn't see his life without me. That well reflects Edward's personality: he was just accustomed, he is a man of habit!"

"Bri, maybe you are being too harsh, that was his way of saying he loves you and wants to marry you! You are missing a chance, after investing one year of your time!

Remember, time is going by fast, too fast."

"I know, Luci, but I can't be in an empty, meaningless relationship. I have made up my mind."

"You are courageous, Bri, you don't have fears of becoming a spinster, not having a family of your own…"

"I don't have those fears. What I fear the most is being caught up in an unfulfilled marriage, facing a hopeless and bleak future.

I wish for love and family like everyone else, of course, but I want it to be right. It still will be challenging, but when we are in unison with the right companion, everything is possible! Happiness is attainable."

"What are you going to do now, Bri? Start over, alone?"

"Edward is leaving for England on Saturday, he is not waiting to go with me in two weeks for the holidays with my family, but he expects me to see him in London and maybe change my mind about us.

That's not going to happen!

I have already made my decision… I'll be moving to Manhattan, enough of commuting. And I thought if you want, Luci, we could be roomies!"

"Oh, Bri, that's the best news you gave me so far! Sure, of course, I am sick and tired of sharing places with others.

We'll be together again, just like old times! I can start looking for an apartment for us right now."

"Do that, Luci. What do you think of Chelsea? David, my boss, mentioned that he lived there when he was single, it is a great area and not far from our office, and I believe not out of the way for your job either. I am thinking of a two bedroom."

"That idea is fabulous, but might be pricey!"

"Don't worry about cost, Luci, I still have the money my Mom left me.

Oh, my Mom! On days like this I miss her even more…"

Sabrina was sad, she sighed.

"Alone again!"

"I am here, Bri, you are not alone, I am not alone, our friendship has carried us this far through everything. I find it amazing that here we are again, old childhood friends starting over, together!

Sorry your heart is broken, but I know how strong you are, you will be alright."

"I will, Luci, I'll be fine, but I am more worried about disappointing my uncle...

My dear Uncle Dimitri had high expectations of me getting married and moving to England. I have to tell him that it was not meant to be...

Just last year I gave him a whole optimistic speech about my future.

I assured him that I was ready for what was to come, I was embracing life and all the possibilities with determination, and today, even broken hearted I feel the same way...

This is not the end, it is a new beginning. Let life happen!

What may be, will be!"

\*\*\*

# ACKNOWLEDGMENTS

Heartfelt thanks to my daughters: Stephanie, for her contributions as my manager and editor, and Samantha, for the perfect cover design.

\*\*\*

Pages 109 and 116 feature lyrics from the ballad "What a Wonderful World," as recorded by Louis Armstrong and written by Bob Thiele and George David Weiss.

# ABOUT THE AUTHOR

M. Carolina Bento is a storyteller who transports her love for other cultures into her family stories.

She believes that a family, as a basic unit of society, in many instances is created not only by biological relatives, but also friends.

From her home around the Washington D.C. area, the author is completing her fifth novel, which in one word will be a *culmination* of her work so far!

www.ingramcontent.com/pod-product-compliance
Lightning Source LLC
Chambersburg PA
CBHW032212170626
46808CB00006B/2439